Forever Always Ends

To Emily Stebner,
Hope you enjoy the book!

Forever Always Ends

Janet VanderMeulen

authorHOUSE®

AuthorHouse™
1663 Liberty Drive
Bloomington, IN 47403
www.authorhouse.com
Phone: 1-800-839-8640

Published by AuthorHouse   04/10/2012

ISBN: 978-1-4685-4310-0 (sc)
ISBN: 978-1-4685-4311-7 (e)

Library of Congress Control Number: 2012900691

CHAPTER 1

"How many times have I told you to knock before you come in here?!" I screamed at my father.

"It's my house and I'll do what I want," he smirked back. "Besides, I have some news for you."

"What? Got a new girlfriend you want me to meet?" I spat.

"Nope. I got a job offer in Philadelphia. We're moving on Monday," he smiled.

"What? That's in a week!"

"Better start packing then."

"Have you ever thought about what I wanted. I have a life here, Dad. I can't just pack up my things and move again! I'm not going!" I argued.

"Oh, yes you are. You are my daughter and you will listen to what I say. I'm you're father and I always will be, whether you like it or not. So you better get used to it."

"This is bullshit! Why couldn't you have died in the crash instead of Mom? She would never have been so self-centered. She would have cared about my feelings!" I said, raising my voice. He moved like a fox. With one swift movement, his calloused hand connected with my pale skin, the pain overwhelming.

"You better watch what you say! I've told you time and time again. Respect me or a slap in the face will be the least of your worries," he yelled back, storming out of the room.

As I looked up to the mirror, my hand reached up, touching my cheek. A tear fell silently; my eyes tracing the faint outline of my father's hand. I sighed and fell back onto my bed. I'm moving again. That meant a new town, new house, new school and new friends. I would have to endure another few months of being the new kid. And the worst part was, I had to say goodbye to my friends in less than a week. At least they weren't really close friends. I hadn't lived in California long enough to have any good friends. I picked up my iPod and cell phone off my night stand and headed out the door. I needed to go somewhere to clear my mind. I headed in the direction of the beach and sped up to a quick jog.

Being away from the house gave me plenty of time to prepare for the upcoming months. If only my mom was here with me so I wouldn't have to deal with my father on my own. He was a self-centered drunk who couldn't care less about my feelings or wants. The only thing that worried him was the idea of being caught. He made sure I knew that. If anyone were to mysteriously find out about his secret life, he would come after me and get rid of me. He would make sure that I could never speak another word. And if that meant killing me, he would do it. Anything to make him feel superior to everyone else. I knew what I had to do. I had to keep everything a secret and keep my mouth shut. And I've done exactly that for the past 6 years, ever since I was 10.

I reached the beach and plopped down on the warm sand. The sun shone brightly and blinded my eyesight. At least I was moving during the summer. It would have been worse moving mid-semester; I would know. I've done it two times so far. Let's just say, it isn't much fun. I laid down on my back and turned my iPod up loud. Closing my eyes, I allowed the music to take me away.

Music. The only reason I had survived living with my father for such a long time. I could just forget my problems for a bit and let the lyrics engulf me. Who knew artists around the world could come up with lyrics that fit my exact mood, whatever the mood may have been. I drifted off to sleep underneath the hot summer sun.

"Hello?" I answered, frantically searching through the sand for my phone after I heard the familiar ringtone.

"Where the hell are you?" I heard my father yell from the other end.

Shit. What time was it. I looked at my watch. Crap! I was supposed to be home to cook supper an hour ago.

"Sorry. I fell asleep at the beach. I'll be home in 10 minutes."

"I really don't care wh-"

Click. I didn't have time to talk. I hung up the phone, picked up my iPod, and sprinted back towards the house.

"Julie!" I heard someone call from the other side of the street. "Where's the fire?"

"I'm supposed to be somewhere, I can't talk," I replied to whoever had asked. I slowed down to a jog when my house came into view. Walking in the front door, I placed my things on the counter and headed to the freezer.

"Dad?" I called out.

"Where were you? I'm starved!" he yelled, emerging from the living room.

"Like I said, I fell asleep at the beach. What do you want to eat?"

"You don't need to cook anything. I already ordered pizza," he replied. "I can never rely on you for anything."

"Whatever," I sighed, walking up to my room. I turned on my computer and checked my facebook; two messages, both from my closest friends back in Seattle. I clicked on the first one. It was from Delilah.

Julie! Hey, long time no speak. How are things going? Did you pass grade 10? Haha, just kidding. Anyway, guess what? Someone actually bought one of my paintings! I got a pretty good price for it too! I am now $350 richer! Hope all is well, Delilah :)

I thought back to the good old times I had with Delilah. She was so amazing. I knew I could always count on her no matter what. We knew everything about each other. The only thing she didn't know was the whole abuse thing. She would not take that to well. I congratulated her on her achievement and told her that I was moving again. I hit send and checked the next one. It was from Carsynn.

Julie, I do believe that we have not talked for a while. It's been a whole . . . week! That is too long my friend! I finally finished that one book I was reading. You should definitely read it. I highly recommend it. It's called Lock & Key incase you forgot. :)

Carsynn, oh Carsynn. Always making my giggle. I replied to her message and then shut my computer off. I headed off to the bathroom to take a much needed shower.

When I finished drying my hair, I headed downstairs to the kitchen to see if the pizza had arrived. Once I was halfway down the staircase, I knew the answer. I could smell the delicious food wafting from the living room. Starving, I grabbed a plate from the cupboard and headed towards the pizza.

"What kind did you get?" I asked as I glanced towards the TV to see what was on.

"It's all gone," my father said, keeping his eyes on the television set. I checked the pizza box to see if he was joking. Not a chance.

"Silly me. Of course it's gone. Since when do you share?" Rolling my eyes, I grabbed my keys, wallet, and phone from the counter and headed out the door. I got into my Chevy truck and headed towards the nearest Subway.

"Hello. What can I get for you?" the guy behind the counter asked.

"Um. Could I get a Foot long Oven Roasted Chicken Breast on Italian Herbs and Cheese?"

"Sure thing. Would you like it toasted?"

"Yes, please," I replied. While my dinner toasted, I listened to an elderly woman in front of me trying to decide what she wanted on her sub.

"Could I get some lettuce on that, please?" she asked.

"Yep," the other employee said.

"Actually, never mind. Better make that some cucumbers and tomatoes."

"Alright," the worker said, taking the lettuce off and throwing it away, replacing it with tomatoes and cucumbers.

"Oh wait, sorry. I meant pickles, not cucumbers. My mistake."

"That's okay," the worker said, slightly annoyed.

"Sorry about the wait," the guy who was helping me said. "What would you like on your sub?"

"Some lettuce, tomatoes, pickles, and cucumbers, please."

"Sure thing."

I noticed that the elderly lady was now at the cash register and was attempting to find exact change for her meal. Boy was I glad I didn't work at places like this. I would not be patient enough for people like that.

"Sauces?"

"Mayonnaise, thanks," I said, opening my wallet.

"Okay, and is that to stay or to go?" the guy asked.

"Uh, let's make it to go," I replied pulling out my 10 dollar bill.

"That'll be $7.53."

I handed the guy my money and grabbed my sub off the counter. "Keep the change," I said as I headed out the door.

I drove home and within 10 minutes, I was back in my bedroom. I dropped my keys and wallet on the night stand and checked my phone for new messages; inbox (0). I shut my phone off and sat on my bed. I turned the radio on, switching the station to Wired 96.5. The music drifted through the room while I enjoyed my amazing sub. It was much better than the stupid pizza that I didn't get to eat, that's for sure.

*   *   *

"Julie!" I heard my father yell for the third time. "We're leaving!"

"Ugh, just give me one second!" I yelled down the stairs. I went back to my room and took one last look around. I checked under the bed and inside the drawers to make sure I hadn't forgotten anything. Picking up the last box on the floor, I headed downstairs, closing the door behind me. I dumped the box into my father's truck and went back to lock the front door of the house. I double checked to make sure I hadn't packed my phone and iPod.

"I wonder who the dumbass was that decided we were driving all the way to Philadelphia?" I thought out loud, taking my seat on the passenger side. Suddenly, I felt the all to familiar pain stretch across my face.

"I told you, don't talk to me like that."

"Ouch! I wasn't talking to you, I was thinking out loud," I said, flipping down the visor and looking in the mirror. "You're lucky I'm wearing cover up because that one is going to show later."

"Maybe I ought to start hitting you somewhere where it won't show then," he said, jabbing me in the side.

"What was that for?" I complained, rubbing my side.

"Your smart-ass attitude."

I glared at my 'father' and turned my iPod on full volume, tuning out whatever it was he was saying. My father started the ignition and pulled out of the driveway and we started our two day journey to the other side of the country. Yay! What a blast this was going to be.

I woke up to the sun shining directly in my face, forcing my eyes shut again. "Where are we?" I asked, half asleep.

No answer.

I shut off the music that was blaring in my ears and looked around the truck.

"Dad?" I asked, opening the passenger door. I stepped out of the truck and looked around. We were parked in front of a huge house. There was a two car garage and I caught a glimpse of what I thought was a pool in the backyard. I went up to the front door and looked through the window. I could see my father sitting on the couch and a few boxes on the ground beside him. I knocked on the door. My father got up from his seat and made his way over, smiling like it was Christmas Day.

"Welcome to your new home!" he exclaimed, ushering me in the door.

"For real? Is the actually our new house?" I asked, bewildered.

"You bet. And you can pick your room. There's three to choose from. There's one downstairs, one on the main floor, and there's one upstairs across from my room," he said, pointing in the direction of all three.

"Uh, I'll go check them out and let you know," I said, starting for the staircase that led downstairs.

I hit the last step and took a look around. My jaw instantly dropped to the ground. This place was even bigger on the inside. The first thing I saw was a huge open area. There was a plasma TV mounted on the wall with couches around the outsides. There were a couple gaming consoles on the shelves with plenty of games to go with them.

I looked around the room hoping to find the door that would lead to my possible room. I headed to one of the doors and opened it up. "That's not it," I laughed as I walked into a bathroom. It was a pretty decent bathroom. It had a bath and shower in it, so I was happy.

I went on to the next door and opened it. Bingo. The first thing I saw was the king size bed on the opposite side of the room. To my right, there was another door. I opened it up and found a walk in closet. "Holy Shit!" I screamed in excitement. I didn't even need to see the other rooms. I knew which one I wanted. This one was secluded, away from my father, and it was nice and cold.

"I'll take this one!" I yelled up the stairs to my father.

"But you haven't even looked at the other rooms," he yelled back.

"Well this one is good enough. I have one question though," I said back.

"What?"

"How can we afford this?"

"I pulled a few strings and we'll manage. And we won't move again for quite some time."

"Good, because I'm pretty sure I'll be happy here. Thanks Dad," I said making my way back up the stairs. I headed out onto the porch to check out the backyard; it was magnificent. As I had suspected there was a pool off to the right side of the yard. A gazebo was set up on the left surrounded by lounging chairs and little tables. I couldn't even imagine what the rest of the house looked like. I headed back through the door and went to the truck to pick up my things. It took me five trips to get all my stuff down to my room. I put everything in its place and headed upstairs to explore the rest of the house.

I spent the majority of the summer tanning in my backyard, staying in touch with friends from everywhere, and surprisingly enough, getting along with my father. He hasn't touched me since that day in the truck, and we've only gotten into five arguments. Most were about him not respecting my privacy. I'd caught him looking through my notebooks in my room once or twice. I ended up hiding everything personal in a box in the back of my closet.

I was laying on a floating device in the pool when my father came out from the house. "School is about to start and we need to get you registered," he said, sitting on the edge of the pool, dipping his feet in.

"Oh, right," I sighed, realizing I had a few months of torture ahead of me.

"Also, I think you should find a job somewhere. I can't keep lending you money until you're eighteen."

Great, a job. How exciting. "I remember seeing a sign at Target asking for help. I'll go there after supper and see if I can get a job," I thought out loud.

"That's a good idea," my father said. He sat on the edge of the pool for two more minutes before getting up and going back into the house.

I grabbed the keys to my truck off the counter. My father had it flown in from California to save on gas and to make sure I made it to Philadelphia. He had a feeling I would take a wrong turn and end up somewhere completely different. My truck roared to life when the key twisted in the ignition. It took me ten minutes to get to the Target.

"Hello. How may I help you?" the lady at the register asked.

"Well I saw the 'Help Wanted' sign out front and I was just wondering who I talk to about applying for the job?"

"Oh, you can speak to me if you like," she smiled. "Do you have a resume?"

"I sure do." I handed her the paper I had been holding.

The lady lead me into a back room and she asked me a few questions about myself. She inquired about wage expectations, available hours, and any other commitments I might have. The interview only took ten minutes and then I was on my way back home.

"I got the job!" I called out as I walked in the front door.

"It's about time," my father grumbled from the couch.

"We're going to the school tomorrow to register me, correct?" I walked into the living room. The overwhelming smell of whiskey hit me like a brick wall.

"You can go on your own, you'll manage," he said, taking another swig.

"You told me you were going to come with me tomorrow."

"I said you can go on your own!" he said, rising to his feet.

Recognizing his behaviour instantly, I decided to stop arguing. "Fine," I replied and hurried downstairs. Turning on my computer, I logged onto my facebook and checked my messages. There was one message. It was from Jonathan, my ex-boyfriend.

Julie. I miss you, I need you. Tell me where you're living now and I'll come pick you up and bring you back to Seattle. I love you.

Damnit. Jonathan was an ex for a reason. I hit reply and typed away.

I told you before Jonathan. We're over. You didn't treat me right. Once a cheater, always a cheater. I'm not telling you where I live and I do not love you. You need to move on.

I hit send and then went to my profile page. "Looks like I haven't updated my status in a while," I laughed and clicked on the little box.

I got a job at the Target today. Going to register for school tomorrow morning. Should be interesting.

I clicked 'Share' and shut down my facebook. *Beep* *Beep* Shit. Where was my cell phone? I followed the sound and found it on the couch outside my room. 1 text message . . . from Jonathan.

To Jonathan: I already told you, I've moved on. Leave me alone.

I sent the message and headed back to my room. Hmm. What to do. "Let's go gaming," I laughed, heading out to the Games Room. I looked at the game systems. What kind of person would just leave these here? My father had told me that the people that lived here earlier no longer had any children living in the house so they left them for the next house owners. We ended up being the lucky recipients. I turned on the closest console and grabbed a game to go along with it. There were pictures of zombies on the front cover. "Well this should be interesting, I sighed as I slid the CD in.

I don't know how long I played the game for, but when I was finished, the light from the sky had gone. I was left in the darkness. I checked my phone and found out it was 12. "Shit. I have to get up early tomorrow." I shut the system off and booked it to my room, changing into my pajamas quickly. I went to my bathroom and brushed my teeth and washed my face. Then I headed off to bed, hoping tomorrow wouldn't be too dreadful.

"My name is Julie Baxton, I'd like to register for the upcoming year," I said, when the secretary looked up from her books.

"Hello Julie, are your parents coming today?" she asked.

"Uh, no. Sorry. My father couldn't make it in today and my mother passed away a while back."

"I'm sorry to hear that, we'll just do this on our own then," she smiled and motioned me towards the office to her right.

I took a seat on the chair closest to the window and settled down for a long meeting. I was asked all sorts of questions; phone number, age, address, my fathers name, the names of all the schools I've been to. This went on for a good two hours. I chose all my courses for the next year and was assigned a locker. I also got a tour of the school so that I wouldn't be completely lost on the first day. I thanked the secretary for all of her help and left the school, happy that I'd gotten that over with. There was one week left of summer holidays and then I would be back here, ready for torture.

I got in my truck and headed home. I didn't have to go to work until school started up. I worked everyday after school except for Tuesdays and Thursdays. I also worked weekends. So that left me with nothing to do for a week, except shop for school supplies.

I got home and grabbed my wallet from my room and headed back out. I drove to the nearest Wal-Mart and bought everything I needed for the school year. Pencils, binders, paper, etc.

Using the self-checkout, I paid for everything and walked out with my hands full. I put my supplies in the back of the truck and drove towards my house. I was half way home when all of a sudden a little dog runs onto the road. I slammed on the brakes as fast as humanly possible.

Janet VanderMeulen

A guy, roughly eighteen years old,ran onto the road and picked up the little, Labrador puppy. The guy waved his apologies at me and smiled; I rolled my eyes. Some people should really invest in leashes. One day their puppy won't be so lucky. Jeez.

CHAPTER 2

"Julie! Get out of the bathroom!" my father shouted from outside the door.

"Just a minute!" I called back.

"Did you finish the milk this morning?" he asked.

"Yeah, I used it with my cereal. It's not that big of a deal. I'll run down to the store and pick up some new milk after school," I said, applying my mascara. My father began slamming on the door. He seriously needed to take some anger management classes. "Calm down Dad! It's just milk. I need to get ready for school. Please leave me alone," I told my father, who was still banging on the door.

"I will not calm down! I need to go to work too. And that is MY milk!"

"Woah! Your milk? Any food in this house is mine too! I live here just like you!" I said, starting to get really annoyed.

"Get out of the bathroom," he fumed.

"Okay, just give me a second. I need to brush my teeth."

"Get out now," he said impatiently. I could tell he was trying to keep his voice down.

I rinsed my mouth with water and spit out what was left of the toothpaste. I unlocked the door as I took one last look in the mirror. All of sudden I saw the door opening quickly in the reflection of the mirror. Before I could react, the door smacked into the side of my forehead and I stumbled backwards. The room began to spin and the light was fading quickly. My body went limp and I fell to the floor, unconscious.

My head was pounding. I could hear my father beside me, asking me if I was okay. I opened my eyes and saw that I was still on the bathroom floor. "What the hell!" I screamed in my fathers face, despite my splitting headache. Then I remembered I had to get to school. "How long was I unconscious for?"

"Only five minutes," my father said, getting up from the floor and going back upstairs.

"Jeez. You are such an ass." I rubbed my head and got up from the floor. I opened the medicine draw and took some pain killers. Hopefully that would lessen the headache somewhat. I looked in the mirror and saw a massive bruise forming where the door had hit me. I had to redo my bangs to hide the mark. I also put extra cover up on to try and hide it. I took one last look in the mirror before I headed upstairs and out the door to my truck.

I drove to the school and parked in the student parking lot. Flipping down the visor, I checked to see if the bruise was sufficiently hidden. The only way the bruise would be seen was if someone went right up to my forehead and inspected it. That was a huge relief. I knew no one would be that close to me today. I was the new kid. Taking a deep breath, I grabbed my backpack from the passenger seat and got out of my truck. There was a sign beside the sidewalk that said, 'Welcome to South Philadelphia High School'. I laughed, more like 'Welcome to Hell'.

I walked through the front doors and found the halls already crowded with students. I headed down the hall where my locker was waiting for me and I chucked my bag into it. People all around me were welcoming each other back and telling stories of the wildest parties during the summer. Covering my face with my hair, I continued walking past all these people and found the office.

"I'd like to pick up my schedule, please," I said to the secretary, who I remembered as the one who registered me.

"Oh Julie, welcome back! How was the rest of your summer?" she asked, all smiles.

"It was great, thanks. I'm sorry, I didn't catch your name," I asked out of curiosity.

"Where are my manners?" She laughed, "my name is Mrs. Pilau."

"That's a cool last name," I smiled.

"Thanks. Anyway, here is your schedule. Good luck." She handed me a piece of paper and smiled.

"Thanks."

I left the office doors and looked at my schedule. First block, English. Second block, Social, Third block, Math. Fourth block, Art. Well at least I started and finished the day off good. I was staring at my schedule, figuring out what time the breaks were when someone ran into me. Or I ran into someone. I'm not sure. Either way, we hit each other and I was on the ground.

"Sorry," I heard someone say as I started to get up. Then a hand reached for me, attempting to help me up.

Accepting the offer, I grabbed it and was hoisted back onto my feet. I looked up at the guy that had ran into me and recognized him immediately. By the look on his face, he recognized me too.

"Hey, you're that girl that I saw driving last week."

"Maybe," I said, "and you're that guy with the cute puppy."

"The one and only," he smiled.

"Get a leash," I spat. "I'd hate to see an adorable puppy die because some irresponsible boy didn't take the time to put a leash on the poor thing." I walked away without waiting for a reply.

There was no way I could deal with any boys. Last time I let myself fall for a boy, my heart was thrown against a wall and shattered into a million pieces. I had to deter any guys that came my way, no matter what. And there was no way I was going to be friends with anyone here. I couldn't bare saying another goodbye when the time came to leave this city for another one far, far away.

Opening my locker, I grabbed a binder and a pencil and headed for what was supposedly my English class. I sat down in the seat farthest from the front. I've learned from past experiences that students couldn't stare at you all class if you were in the back. And if they did turn around to catch a glimpse of the new kid, the teacher would see them and tell them to turn around. The system was fool proof. I took the seat in the corner, minimizing the number of people sitting around me. I watched as a shy looking girl took a seat next to me. She was roughly 5'9 with long, straight, blonde hair. She was wearing skinny jeans and a purple hoodie. She looked over me and gave me a small smile and turned back to the front.

The bell rang and the rest of the class began to file in. The intercom came on overhead and welcomed everyone back and wished everyone a successful school year. Announcements were made regarding school committees and sports teams. Once that was over, I prepared myself for the introduction of the new kid. No sooner had this thought crossed my mind when the teacher stood up and called my name, asking me to raise my hand. I did so, reluctantly. All the eyes turned to stare at me. I made sure that my bangs were covering the right side of my face. I gave a weak smile as everyone collected their first impression of me. Hopefully it wasn't that bad of an impression. The teacher then proceeded to inform the class where I had come from and why I had moved to Philadelphia. I sighed in relief when the last pair of eyes returned to the front of the class. The teacher began to go over the course outline for the semester.

"Psst," I heard from somewhere on the right. Looking over, I found the girl beside me had a note in her hand that she wanted me to take. I took the piece of paper and unfolded it as quietly as I could. The note said:

Hey, welcome to Philadelphia. The names Ella. I saw that you applied at Target. I work there too. See you there :)

I folded the paper up and put it in my pocket. Great. I made a friend. That's exactly what I didn't want to do. Well looks like it was too late now, because turns out I worked with her. Might as well make the best of it. I looked over at Ella and smiled at her. I made a mental note to thank her later for reaching out. Maybe I did need a friend or two to get through this year. If I still lived here by the end of it, that is.

I sat through the rest of the lesson, trying to dismiss the headache that was slowly creeping its way back into my head.

Finally the bell rang, and I headed out the door after acknowledging a few 'Hey's and 'Hi's'. I got to my locker and threw my binder in. I then switched it for the next binder I needed. I pulled my schedule out of my pocket and scanned it, looking for the next place I needed to be. Picking up my binder and pencil, I headed off to the social room. Once again, I picked the seat in the far back corner of the class. And just like the English class, students began filing in after the bell rang. I was looking at the posters on the wall when I heard someone sit down beside me.

"Hey," said a familiar voice.

"Can you not take a hint?" I asked without looking at the guy.

"Not really. The names Luke," he laughed, sticking his hand out, expecting me to shake it.

I looked over at him and ignored the hand shake that was expected. I just turned my gaze to the front and payed attention to the lecture the teacher was giving about having no cellphones in class. Apparently, if a teacher saw you with your cell phone during class, you would get it taken away for the rest of the day. And then your parents would have to pick it up at the office.

"Psst," I heard yet again for the second time today.

"What?" I whispered over to Luke.

"What's your name?" he whispered back.

"Julie."

"That's a really pretty na-"

"Excuse me, do you have something you would like to share with the class? It seems to me that it is more interesting than what we're talking about up here," the teacher said, glaring directly at Luke and I. "Enlighten us, why don't you."

"Sorr-" I began to say.

"Well you see, Mr. Culter. This here, beside me, is Julie. And it seems like you forgot to introduce her to the class."

"Oh, you're right. Julie, why don't you come up here and say a few words?" the teacher smirked.

"Thanks a lot," I whispered sarcastically.

"My pleasure," Luke smiled.

I got up to the front and all eyes were staring at me. "Well, uh. My name is Julie Baxton. I moved here from California in the middle of the summer because my dad got a job offer here." I started to make my way back to my seat when the teacher motioned for me to stay up there.

"It seems that young Luke over there has a question for you," Mr. Culter said, gesturing towards the back of the room.

I glared at Luke, "yes?"

"When's your birthday?"

"Sorry?" I asked, thrown off by the question.

"I said, when is your birthday?"

"June 27th," I said, making my way to my seat, not stopping for any questions this time. "I hate you," I whispered when I was back in my chair.

The rest of the class went by smoothly, except for a few whispers from Luke, which I ignored. Finally, the bell rang which meant it was lunch time. I headed out of the class as fast as I could, hoping to get away from Luke. Regardless of my efforts, he still managed to catch up with me.

"Hey, Julie. I'm sorry if I embarrassed you," he said, stepping in front of me so that I had to respond.

"I wasn't embarrassed," I glared, stepping around him.

My locker was just around the corner from the social room. I unlocked it, and dumped my binder inside. I grabbed my sandwich and turned around to see Luke still standing there. "What?" I asked, slightly annoyed.

"You want to sit with me at lunch today?" he said, too innocently.

"No. I'll be fine," I said, laughing at the thought of sitting with Luke. Entering the cafeteria, I sat down at one of the smaller tables and started munching on my ham sandwich.

"Well if you don't want to sit with me, I'll sit with you," I heard from behind. I rolled my eyes. This kid did not give up easily.

Luke took a seat beside me and dug into his homemade lasagna. "Don't look so glum," he laughed, "it's better than sitting by yourself."

As much as I hated Luke, he was right. At least it looked like I wasn't a complete loner. My phone had been sitting on the table when Luke noticed it and picked it up.

"Excuse me?" I said, trying to snatch it back, "I do believe that belongs to me."

"Oh really?" he asked, acting like he didn't know. He pushed a few buttons before passing it back to me, "sorry about that, I thought it was mine. We must have the same phone. We have something in common!"

"Oh, gag me with a spoon," I said, as I took the last bite of my sandwich.

Math class was the worst out of all the classes I'd had so far today. The teacher constantly asked me for answers to questions he was asking. Clearly Mr. Portau didn't understand the hand raising system. Last time I checked, if a student didn't raise their hand, they clearly did not know the answer. Yet, teachers always asked the students with their hands down for answers. This always left the more eager students disappointed that their name wasn't called. Maybe you should ask them for the answer and then everyone would be happy, just saying. By the end of the class, I had been called upon six times. And each time I just mumbled something incoherent to anyone and eventually the teacher moved on and picked on someone else. The bell rang and I booked it for my next class. No way was I staying in that room longer than I needed to. I hated math and I'm pretty sure math hated me.

I found my art class just as the bell rang. I scanned the room for an empty chair and spotted one in the corner. Lucky me, I thought. I glanced to the people surrounding the seat and noticed Ella sitting quietly to the left, in her own desk. I sat down next to her and quietly whispered, "sorry for leaving English so soon, I didn't want to be late for my next class."

"It's okay, I understand," she whispered as the teacher got up and got the class under control.

"Welcome to Art 20, my name is Mrs. Pokis, for those of you who don't know me," she glanced at me and smiled. Mrs. Pokis then started handing out papers which explained what the rules and expectations were. She handed a few more sheets out that explained the different types of projects we would be working on.

I loved art. It was one of the places where I could express my inner feelings freely. It was the one other thing besides music where I could escape from the world for a bit. I always considered myself an artistic person. Delilah had told me on many occasions that I should try and sell some of my pieces like her. I liked looking at my artwork and kept them hung up on my bedroom wall. Maybe one day

I would consider selling them, but right now, they're my comfort pieces. They're apart of who I am. I can't just sell pieces of me to complete strangers. It didn't feel right.

"Julie," I felt someone nudge my side. I looked over and saw Ella with an expectant gaze. I gave her a questioning look. "The teacher is talking to you." Oh! I turned my gaze to Mrs. Pokis.

"Sorry, could you please repeat that?" I asked, wondering what she could possibly want.

"Julie, please pay attention. I was just wondering if you could say a little something about yourself, now that everyone is settled down."

"Oh, sure. My name is Julie Baxton and I moved here from California with my dad when he got offered a job here," I finished off.

"Have you taken any art lessons before?" Mrs. Pokis asked.

"No, not really. I've only worked on a few projects during my free time," I replied. Mrs. Pokis nodded in approval and moved on to answer some kid's question. He had been standing behind Mrs. Pokis the whole time, tapping his foot. Some people were so impatient.

"Julie!" I heard Luke holler from behind me, "wait up!"

I rolled my eyes and kept walking. Luke ran up behind me and matched my pace. "You don't give up, do you?"

"Giving up gets you nowhere," he laughed, "and where are you headed?"

"To work," I sighed. Might as well just get used to this. I had a feeling Luke would be a common sight from now on.

"Oh really, where do you work?" he asked, actually sounding legitimately interested.

"Just down the street at Target."

"Hey! I work at Blockbuster just down the street from there," he smiled. "Looks like we can walk to work together whenever we both work."

"Yippee," I said sarcastically, giving Luke two thumbs up and plastering a huge smile on my face. "All my hopes and dreams, finally coming true!"

"Oh, so you're dreaming about me, are you?" he laughed, poking me in the side.

"I don't think that's really possible. We met today, and I haven't slept yet. Jeez. Please try and use your brain once in a while," I sighed, pointing at his head.

"Ah, you got me there," he laughed. "I'll just ask you the same question tomorrow."

"Don't get your hopes up," I said as I reached the Target.

"See you later Jules!" Luke called out as he continued down the street.

Great, I have a nickname.

Work went by so slowly. What felt like ten years turned out to be only five measly hours. I found out Ella worked on opposite days of me. We only worked together Fridays and Saturdays.

I stepped out of the Target at nine o'clock and started walking back down the street to pick up my truck from the school parking lot. I left it at the parking lot because I didn't really feel the necessity to drive two blocks so I just walked to work. When I got back to my truck, I plopped my bag on the passenger seat and headed home.

When I got inside my house, I went straight downstairs to my room and fell back onto my bed. I was so tired and my head was still throbbing. I got up and looked in the mirror hanging on my wall. I swept my bangs back to look at the bruise that was more visible now than it was this morning. Thank god I had bangs to cover it up. I went upstairs and grabbed an Advil from the medicine cabinet. Raiding the fridge, I found some left over spaghetti from last nights supper and warmed it up in the microwave.

Back downstairs, I sat on my bed, enjoying my food. I jumped when my phone vibrated in my pocket. I read the text.

To Julie:
From Dad:
I won't be home for the next week. I left on a business trip. I'll be back Saturday.

I couldn't believe it. He just got up and left for an entire week without telling me beforehand. What an ass. Then I remembered about the incident at lunch. I looked through my phone and found a new contact listed. Of course.

To Luke:
From Julie:
Why did you put your number in my phone??

I hit send and not even 2 minutes later, I felt my phone vibrating again.

To Julie:
From Luke:
I decided you might need it :)

Oh jeez, really?

To Luke:
From Julie:
And if I delete it?

To Julie:
From Luke:
I'll keep texting you, because I now have your number

To Luke:
From Julie:
Whatever, I'm going to bed.

To Julie:
From Luke:
Sweet dreams ;)

I couldn't help but smiling. I plugged my phone into my charger and headed off to bed.

CHAPTER 3

My eyes darted across the room, looking for him. He was no where to be found. But then I spotted him, leaning against one of the cars in the parking lot. I just stood there, staring at his beauty. He was roughly 6'1 with dirty blonde hair. His hair was just the right length. It was long, but not that long that you couldn't see his face. The longest strand barely passed his ears. It was a nice shaggy look. His body was perfectly toned with a light tan kissing his skin. He noticed me standing there and smiled slightly. Our eyes locked for what seemed like ages and then he looked back at his friends. God, those eyes. They were so beautiful. His baby blue eyes had the power to melt me away. I don't know what made me do it, but my feet started moving towards this god-like figure. He must have seen me coming, because he too, started walking towards me, leaving his friends. Our eyes met as we approached each other. We stopped walking when there was half a meter between us. We just stared at each for ages. His baby blue eyes meeting my blue-green ones. Then something happened. He moved closer to me, sweeping a piece of hair out of my eyes. He leaned in slowly, making sure I was okay with everything. I closed my eyes and leaned in too.

My hand flew through the air and slammed the snooze button. I was brought back to reality and then I remembered the dream. Shit. I had dreamt about him. It was his fault though. He was the one that brought the idea to my head.

I decided I might as well start getting ready for school and hopped into the shower. I took my time, knowing that my father wasn't home to yell at me for taking too long. Forty-five minutes later, I was showered, clothed, and fed. I went back down to the bathroom to style my hair and apply my make up. I swept my bangs to the side and saw my bruise. It was a dark purple-blue colour. I would need quite a bit of cover up to hide this. I applied my cover up and mascara and then started on my hair. I blow dried my hair and then straightened it. I made sure the bruise was covered fully by my hair. I decided to put a small braid on the left side of my head as well. I took a look in the mirror. I looked like an ordinary girl. "Perfect," I smiled.

I unplugged my phone from the charger and saw it had one unread message.

To Julie:
From Luke:
Morning :)

I rolled my eyes. Such a go-getter. There was no way I would be able to get rid of this boy. I could still try though.

To Luke:
From Julie:
Don't you have someone else to annoy??

To Julie:
From Luke:
Absolutely no one. Plus, you're adorable when you're annoyed ;)

To Luke:
From Julie:
Jesus, such a charmer.

To Julie:
From Luke:
I think you sent that message to the wrong person. My name is Luke, not Jesus :P

I read that last message and laughed. A charming comedian. Just what I needed. I put my cell phone in my pocket and headed out the front door.

I entered the school at around 8:45. My timing was perfect. I had enough time to stop at my locker and then make my way to English. I took my seat in the back and opened up my books, waiting for class to end. I felt my phone buzz in my pocket.

To Julie:
From Luke:
You look great today :)

Jeez, I couldn't help but smile. At least he hadn't come up to me and started up a conversation. I looked up and saw Ella take a seat in her desk beside me.

"Good morning," she smiled. "How are you?"

"I'm great, thanks. And yourself?"

"I'm pretty good too."

"Hey, can I sit with you at lunch today?" I asked.

"Sure thing. You want my number so we can find each other?" she asked, pulling out her phone.

"That would be great," I smiled, taking my phone out again.

We exchanged numbers just as the bell rang. We took that as our cue to put our phones away. I didn't want to have mine taken away on the second day.

English went by quickly. Ms. Doril was talking about the formal format of an essay, something teachers seemed to teach every year. But I loved English, so it didn't really matter to me. Unlike most people, I enjoyed writing essays. I enjoyed writing in general.

Before I knew it, I was sitting in social beside Luke, who would not stop talking. Every time Luke would whisper something, Mr. Culter would shoot us a glare. This glare would keep Luke quiet for about . . . two minutes, if that.

"So," he whispered when Mr. Culter turned his back, "what did you dream about?"

"Nothing," I whispered back.

"Really?" Luke asked, leafing through some papers.

"Yep," I smiled.

"Too bad I don't believe you," Luke laughed.

"I didn't!" I said as quietly as I could.

"You dreamt about me, I know it."

"No I didn't," I sighed.

"Why are you so defensive then?" he laughed.

I didn't have a chance to answer the question because Mr. Culter had interrupted. "Mr. Hecks. Do you have something to share with the class?"

"No sir," Luke smiled.

"Pay attention then," Mr. Culter spat, turning back to the white board.

"Yes Sir," Luke sighed, slouching in his seat.

"Do you always have a habit of following people around?" I asked, seeing Luke walking beside me after class.

"Nope," he laughed, "just you."

"I'm honoured," I said sarcastically.

"You should be," he smiled.

"And another thing?" I asked.

"Hmm?"

"Does Mr. Culter hate you or something?"

"Probably."

"I could tell," I laughed. I stopped at my locker and dropped my books off. Luke must have left to drop his things off because he was no where to be found. I took advantage of this and made a dash for the cafeteria. I sat down at the same lunch table as yesterday and pulled out my phone.

To Ella:
From Julie:
Where are you?

"Hey loner," I heard Luke say behind me. He sat down and I punched him in the shoulder. Looks like my plan didn't work. It was impossible to get rid of this kid.

"I am not a loner, I have someone who's coming to join me today," I sighed.

"You don't like sitting with me?" he asked, putting on his best pouting face.

"Nope," I said. "Not at all."

"Well I'll just sit here with you and your new friend," he said, proud that he'd thought of the idea.

"Only if it's okay with her," I said, rolling my eyes. My phone vibrated and a checked the text.

To Julie:
From Ella:
I'm sitting at the booth to your right.

I looked up and sure enough, I saw Ella waving me over to a table full of people. She patted the seat beside her and motioned for me to come over. I got up and looked at Luke, "I don't know if there's room for you."

"I'll pull up a chair," he said, not backing down.

I got over to the table and sat down. I whispered in Ella's ear, "Luke is kind of stalking me and he wants to sit with us." I laughed as he picked up a chair and proceeded to trip over a different one.

"Oh, you're going to have to tell me about this later," she whispered back.

"Anyway, everyone meet Julie. Julie, meet Nicole, Mike, Justin, Jessi, and Chris." She pointed at each friend as she said there name.

"Hey guys," I said, waving at them. They all smiled back and waved.

"Hey Ella, nice to meet you," Nicole smiled from across the table.

I studied their faces. Each of them were in at least one of my classes. Nicole and Justin were in my Social class, Mike and Jessi were in my Math class, and Chris was in my Art class. I recognized him as the one that sat a row in front of where Ella and I sat.

Just then, Luke pulled up his chair he'd gotten and plopped it down beside me.

"Hey guys," he smiled, taking a bite of his slice of cheese pizza.

Everyone gave Ella and I a questioning look and Ella just waved it away, meaning she would explain later. "So Luke, how did you meet Julie?" Ella asked, rather curious as to how the popular guy in school was stalking me.

"Well," he said, swallowing his last bite, "it all started when she almost hit my dog with her car."

"Your dog ran on the road," I said defensively. "Buy a leash and maybe it won't happen."

"And then we bumped into each other in the hallway on the first day of school. She almost bit my head off when she recognized me," he laughed, roughing up my hair.

Shit. I quickly moved my bangs back in front of my bruise, hoping no one saw it. I fixed the rest of my hair and punched Luke in the shoulder again.

"Ouch, Julie that hurts. Please don't do it again," he laughed, rubbing his shoulder.

"Grow a pair," I said as I went back to eating my lunch. Everyone else had finished and was talking amongst each other.

We were sitting in art class, practising different shading techniques. "Spill," Ella whispered, wanting to know more about Luke.

"Well, there's not much to say, I've tried getting rid of him but nothing I do does the trick. If anything it makes him come closer," I shrugged, sharpening my pencil.

"Wait, what?" she asked. "You're trying to get rid of him. Are you crazy?!"

"No. Why?"

"You're talking about Luke Hecks. Sweetest guy at Philadelphia High."

"So?"

"The point is, he never goes after girls. There was only one other girl he was interested in, but she moved away just before things got serious. So what I'm saying is, give him a chance. Try and be friendly," she laughed, giving me a nudge. As much as I hated to hear this, she was probably right. So, looks like nice Julie was coming to visit for a while.

The final bell rang and I headed over to my locker. I turned the corner and saw Luke standing there, waiting.

"Hey," I said, reaching for my lock. "What's up?"

"Do you work tonight?" he asked casually.

"Nope. I have the night off."

"Oh darn. I guess I'm walking by myself today," he pouted, walking towards the exit.

"You want a ride?" I called back, stopping Luke in his tracks.

He turned around and skipped back to my locker. "That would be lovely," he said in the worst English accent I had ever heard.

We got to the student parking lot and found my truck. I got in the drivers seat while Luke literally jumped into the passenger seat. "A little excited, are we?" I laughed as I shifted into reverse.

"Of course!" he smiled. He looked like a four year old on Christmas morning. It only took two minutes for us to get to Blockbuster. I parked close to the front door.

"Hey Jules?" Luke asked, turning to look me in the eyes.

"Yes?"

"I'm throwing a party this weekend and I was wondering if-"

"If I want to come?" I asked, finishing his sentence.

"Exactly," he smiled.

"I'll have to make sure I'm not working, but I'll try and make it. Friday night?" I asked.

"You bet," he laughed, plastering his four year old smile back on his face. He got out of the truck and waved goodbye before entering the store. I waved back and left the parking lot.

"What a character," I laughed.

I got home around 3:45 and decided to watch a movie. I didn't have any homework yet since it was only the second day of school. I dropped my bag on the kitchen floor and headed downstairs. I sat cross legged in front of the shelves with all the movies. That was another thing left behind by the previous family. There were hundreds of movies on these shelves. After five minutes of browsing, I decided on the Pink Panther. I had never seen this movie but I heard it was really funny. My friends back in Seattle had reenacted scenes from this movie so many times, I figured I should probably watch it. I put the movie in the DVD player and went upstairs to find some food.

I decided to pop some popcorn. It was always a suitable food choice for movies. You could never go wrong with popcorn at hand. As I waited for the popcorn to pop, I pulled out my phone and texted Ella.

To Ella:
From Julie:
You wanna come over and watch a movie? lol

I hit send and went downstairs to make myself comfortable. I felt my phone vibrate and I looked at the text.

To Julie:
From Ella:
Yes! Of course! Where do you live?

To Ella:
From Julie:
Okay cool. I don't really know how to describe where I live. Wanna meet up at the school?

To Julie:
From Ella:
Yah sure, I'll be there in 10 min.

With that, I headed upstairs and out the door. I was at the school within 15 minutes. "Sorry, I live a little further than you do," I apologized when I saw her leaning against her vehicle. "Do you want to follow in your car, or car pool?"

"I'll just follow, and I'll remember where I'm going so I can come straight to your house next time," she laughed as she got in her car. I got back in mine and headed back home. I made sure she was still following incase I lost her. That wouldn't be all to great. We reached my house and I invited Ella inside. I walked over to the fridge and grabbed a can of coke.

"You want something?" I asked turning around to face Ella.

Her jaw had dropped when she saw my house. "This place is huge!" she said, spinning herself around so she could see everything.

"Uh, yeah. Kind of," I laughed. I grabbed Ella a can of coke and headed down the stairs, while Ella followed, still gaping at the beauty of my house.

When Ella had finally come back down to planet Earth, she started asking me questions about Luke again. "How was your ride with him after school," she laughed. Obviously she had seen us get into the same vehicle.

"Well, he asked me to go to his party this weekend," I said casually.

"Actually? Sweet deal!" she nodded her head in approval.

"Yah, I guess so. You want to come with me, so I won't be all by myself?" I asked, already knowing the answer.

"Of course I will!" she smiled, overjoyed at the thought.

Ella ended up leaving around 8:30 because she had to get back home before her parents got worried. I thanked her for coming and closed the door after her.

We had laughed for hours after the movie ended, impersonating the main character and his crazy antics. We ordered pizza for supper and just sat around and talked for a while. I found out that she had moved to Philadelphia two years ago. I told her all about my other schools, and homes, and friends. I told her about my friends Carsynn & Delilah back in Seattle. I also told Ella about all our adventures we had. And in turn, Ella told me all about her old town and old friends. She talked a lot about her new friends as well. It turns out, Ella likes Chris . . . a lot. They had been friends ever since Ella moved here in grade 9. I think they would look cute together, but that's just my opinion. Ella told me that Chris would never go out with her; that they would always stay just friends. I had a feeling that could change with a little effort.

A wave of exhaustion fell over me and I decided to go take a shower and headed off to bed.

My eyes darted across the room, looking for him. He was no where to be found. But then I spotted him, leaning against one of the cars in the parking lot. I just stood there, staring at his beauty. He was roughly 6'1 with dirty blonde hair. His hair was just the right length. It was long, but not that long that you couldn't see his face. The longest strand barely passed his ears. It was a nice shaggy look. His body was perfectly toned with a light tan kissing his skin. He noticed me standing there and smiled slightly. Our eyes locked for what seemed like ages and then he looked back at his friends. God, those eyes. They were so beautiful. His baby blue eyes had the power to melt me away. I don't know what made me do it, but my feet started moving towards this god-like figure. He must have seen me coming, because he too, started walking towards me, leaving his friends. Our eyes met as we approached each other. We stopped walking when there was half a meter between us. We just stared at each for ages. His baby blue eyes meeting my blue-green ones. Then something happened. He moved closer to me, sweeping a piece of hair out of my eyes. He leaned slowly, making sure I was okay with everything. I closed my eyes and leaned in too.

I sat up in bed, out of breath. Damnit! I did it again.

CHAPTER 4

The next two days flew by like nothing. Before I knew it, it was Friday afternoon. The final bell was about to ring and I would be out of here for the weekend. I sat in my seat, counting down the minutes till the bell rang. Five minutes left. I was excited for the party tonight. It started around 7:00. That gave me three and a half hours to waste. Four minutes left. I could tell that Ella was excited too. I had told Luke that I was bringing a friend. He had agreed, no persuading needed. Three minutes. I had hung out with Ella and Luke all week. I had met Ella's friends, and tonight at the party, I was going to meet Luke's friends. They had been on a road trip all week and were coming back tonight. Luke was supposed to be on the road trip but couldn't get time off work. So he stayed home. Two minutes left. I started to pack up all my supplies. I had been working on a collage portraying life in general. I was almost finished, I just needed to put the final touches on. One minute to go. I got up and stacked my chair in the back of the room with all the others. I grabbed my things and stood by the door. Ella came and stood beside me. We were both going to my house after school to get ready for the party. 15 seconds. I kept my eyes on the clock. 10 seconds. Ella was staring at the clock too. 5 seconds.

"Finally!" I laughed, pulling Ella along when the bell rang. Our lockers happened to be in the same general area. We counted at one point. There were only 13 lockers in between hers and mine. I got to my locker and shoved my books in. I grabbed my math text book and shoved it in my bag. Mr. Portau decided to assign 30 questions in math that were due on Monday. Yay! I shut my locker and headed over to Ella's locker.

"You excited?" she asked when I leaned against a locker, waiting for her.

"You bet!" I smiled, "I get to meet Luke's friends tonight."

"Awe," she cooed.

"What?" I asked.

"You like him, don't you?"

"No."

"Sure," she laughed, "whatever makes you sleep at night." Ella shut her locker door and we headed for the parking lot, getting into my truck.

"I do not like him," I said, trying to defend myself.

"Yup. Okay Julie," Ella said sarcastically. I sighed, knowing I would have to convince her later. I pulled out of the parking lot and headed home.

Ella and I started getting ready at 5:45. I hopped in the shower while Ella went through my closet, picking something out for me to wear. When I got out of the bathroom, I found an outfit laid out on my bed. Ella must have gone to take a shower upstairs because she was no longer downstairs. I looked at what she had found. My strapless red top had been matched up with my dark blue skinnies. A pair of black flats had been placed on the bed. Closing the bedroom door, I quickly changed into the outfit and headed upstairs to look for something to eat. I took some pizza out of the freezer and put it in the oven. I went back downstairs and started blow drying my hair. I caught a glimpse of the bruise from Monday. It was a brownish colour and was disappearing. Thank god for that. When I finished blow drying my hair, I put on my makeup, still unsure of what to do with my hair.

"Shit," I said, remembering the pizza in the oven. I ran upstairs and took it out of the oven. It was perfect, just really hot. I set it on the counter to let it cool. "Ella! Dinner is served," I yelled, hoping she would hear me.

"Okay! I'll be right there," she yelled back. I got the pizza cutter and started cutting up the pizza. Ella emerged from the bathroom and we started eating the pizza, blowing on the pizza to try and cool it down a bit.

"I really like that on you," Ella said, pointing at my ensemble.

"Well thank you," I smiled, clearing the table of our dishes and left over food. We both headed back downstairs and Ella applied her make up while I put my hair up into a messy bun. After debating for 10 minutes, Ella finally decided to straighten her hair and leave it down. By the time we had finished getting ready, it was already 8:30.

"Whoops, we have to go," I said, pointing at the clock. "We're going to be late."

"Ah, that's fine," Ella laughed, grabbing her phone from her back pack and putting it in her pocket. I grabbed mine and texted Luke.

To Luke:
From Julie:
We need directions to your place.

Within minutes, I received a text back. We got into my truck and drove to Luke's. It only took 10 minutes. Looks like he didn't live that far away. It wasn't hard to find his house. You could hear the music blaring 5 houses down and people were sitting on the front lawn. I parked my car across the street and stepped out of the truck. Ella came up and stood beside me.

"Ready?" she asked.

"Ready," I said, taking the first step towards the party inside.

I opened the front door to find myself greeted by some type of dubstep remix. I shook my head, hoping some better music would play soon. My phone started vibrating and I took it out and read the text.

To Julie:
From Luke:
And you finally show up :P

I looked up to see Luke walking towards Ella and I. He reached us and gave me a big bear hug. He said hello to Ella and then grabbed my hand and pulled me into the living room. I gave Ella a glance and she nodded, shooing me away with hand gestures. I made a mental note to find her later. There was no way I was ditching her tonight. I looked forward, trying to keep up with the eager Luke. I was probably going to meet his buddies.

Sure enough, within two minutes, I was surrounded by his best friends.

"Julie meet my best buddies, Mark and Jake." He pointed to each of his buddies as their names were said. "Guys, meet Julie."

"Damn Luke, you weren't joking, she is good looking," the one named Jake said, nodding in approval. I looked over to see Luke balling his fists up and glaring at Jake.

"Awe! Luke thinks I'm good looking," I laughed.

Luke smiled at me and I detected a slight rosiness in his cheeks. He was so adorable sometimes. Wait, what did I just say? Adorable? What was I thinking? This was not a part of the plan. I was beginning to think that Ella was right.

"I'll deal with you later," Luke laughed, pulling me towards the kitchen. "Want a drink?"

"Sure," Mark piped up.

"I wasn't talking to you," Luke laughed, "I was talking to Julie."

"I'll have a beer!" Mark called anyway. Luke waved backwards and we walked into the kitchen.

"I'll have a vodka and coke," I smiled, reaching for a plastic cup from the counter.

"Alrighty, one vodka and coke coming up," Luke smiled, grabbing my cup. He mixed my drink and passed it to me while he grabbed two beers from the fridge. One for him and one for Mark. We walked back to the living room and I saw Ella sitting on the couch with Chris. They were talking and laughing, having a great time. I couldn't help but smile at the sight of them. We got back to Mark and Jake, who were playing a drinking game with some girls.

"I win!" Jake yelled, getting up and doing a victory dance.

"Whatever dude, I almost beat you this time," Mark yelled back. I took a sip from my cup. It was really strong but damn did it taste good. I had gone to a few parties here and there when I was living in my old towns. Vodka and coke was my favourite drink. Occasionally I would have a cooler. Those were pretty decent too.

"Luke, buddy! Come join us," Mark said, waving him over, "and bring my beer!"

I laughed as I pushed Luke towards the boys. With drink in hand, I walked over to Ella, who was laughing at a joke Chris had said.

"Hey Julie," Chris smiled, patting a seat beside him. I took the seat and looked over at Ella, who was blushing.

"Hey Ella, sorry about earlier. Luke wanted me to meet his buddies," I laughed, gesturing towards the huddle of guys, chanting "Chug! Chug! Chug!"

"Don't worry about it Julie, I found Chris right away."

"So you and Luke?" Chris smirked.

"Not even close," I said, as casually as possible.

"Seems pretty close to me," Chris smiled. Ella started whistling a little tune.

"You told him," I shot towards Ella.

"So it is true! I knew it," Chris shouted.

Damn. I should have kept my mouth shut. "Since you seem to think you know everything, lets get the facts straight. I do not like Luke. He follows me everywhere and we ended up becoming friends. That's all it is, nothing more."

"Mhm, sure," Chris said, laughing. I rolled my eyes and got up from the couch.

"Ella, do you want a drink?" I asked, motioning for her to follow.

"Oh, that would be nice," she said, following my lead. We headed into the kitchen and I set my cup on the counter. "Is there any ice tea in here?" Ella asked, opening the fridge.

"Not drinking?" I asked.

"Ah, found some," Ella smiled, "and to answer your question, no. I don't really enjoy drinking too much."

"Oh, alright," I said, taking a seat on one of the stools. "So Ella, I have some news for you."

"Spill," she said, hoisting herself on the stool beside me.

I sat on the stool beside her and took a deep breath in. "I think I'm falling for Luke."

"Called it!" Ella screamed, "I am a genius."

"Okay Ella, whatever makes you sleep at night," I laughed, taking another drink from my cup.

"Don't deny it. I so knew what was going on," she said, pointing her finger at me.

"Wow Bessy, simmer down," I laughed, "I know you knew. It was the genius part that threw me off."

"Ha. Ha. You're so funny," Ella said sarcastically, taking a sip from her cooler.

"Hello there ladies," I heard the familiar voice from behind me.

"Hi Luke," I said, not turning around.

"Uh, I got to go. Chris wanted me to bring him a beer," Ella lied, getting up from the couch. She left the room.

"I thought he wanted a beer," Luke laughed, noticing she had left without a beer.

"She'll realize it soon enough," I laughed, going along with her lie.

"Yah, I guess so. Do you think she'll be back right away?" Luke asked, glancing at the doorway.

"Probably not," I laughed, finishing off my drink. "Why?"

"I was just wondering," he shrugged, glancing at my empty cup. "Do you want another one?"

"Oh, sure," I said, passing him my cup, "I like it when you make them."

"So I've been told," he laughed, mixing my drink. "So what do you think of my friends? Pretty retarded, right?"

"They kind of remind me of you," I laughed, sticking my tongue out.

"Ouch. That hurt, right in the feel-bads," he pouted, pointing at his heart.

"Suck it up, princess," I laughed, taking a sip of the new drink Luke had handed to me.

"Ooh, you're going to pay for that," Luke laughed, making his way towards me.

"As if you could catch me," I laughed, getting up from the bar stool and booking it out the kitchen. Clearly that wasn't such a good idea because within seconds, Luke was behind me, grabbing my waist, and pulling me back towards him.

"Gotcha," he whispered in my ear.

"No fair," I pouted, setting my drink on a nearby table.

He spun me around so that I was facing him. He looked into my eyes with his beautiful, baby blue eyes. My heart rate sped up. I thought it was going to jump right out of my chest. I could hear it beating loudly in my ears. Oh god. I hoped Luke couldn't hear it. He leaned in and I could smell is cologne. I couldn't quite make out what kind it was, but it smelled amazing. I gazed into his eyes and he started to move closer. Oh god. Was he going to do what I thought he was going to do? He moved in even closer so we were centimetres apart. I closed my eyes.

"C'mon," he whispered, "let's party."

Oh my god. Really? Now I just felt like a complete loser.

Luke grabbed my hand and dragged me over to where Jake and Mark were sitting, still playing drinking games.

"Alright Jules, let's see what you're made of," Luke smiled, passing me a beer.

"Beer? Really?" I asked, disgusted by the thought of drinking it.

"You bet," Luke laughed, "let's see who can chug a beer the fastest between you, Jake, Mark, and me."

We took a seat beside Mark and Jake and got ready. Some guy in the back started counting down, "3,2,1, Go!"

We all grabbed our beers and started chugging. The taste was awful but I kept going. My first goal was to finish the beer. My second was to beat at least one of the guys. I finished it off and set my empty can on the table in front of me just as Luke did the same. Mark and Jake set their empties down shortly after.

"Looks like we tied," I laughed, feeling the alcohol hit my system.

"Well there has to be a winner, so we'll do it again," Luke laughed, passing me another beer.

"Ugh, really? Can't we do it with something else? This beer tastes like shit," I said, eyeing up my Vodka and Coke on the table.

Luke followed my stare and laughed, "alright, but that stuff is a shit load stronger than this beer." He got up and went to the kitchen to fetch three more Vodka and Coke's. I got up and grabbed mine from the table.

"Dang Julie, you sure finished that one off fast," I heard Jake chuckle from the left.

"Guys, I have partied before," I said, spotting Ella sitting with Chris again. She saw me too and I waved her and Chris over.

"Hey Julie, what's up?" Ella smiled, looking at the guys who were giggling away. I know, they were giggling. How cool were they?

"I want you to meet Jake and Mark, Luke's friends. Guys, this is Ella and Chris," I said, gesturing towards my friends.

"What's up?" Mark smiled, while Jake nodded his head.

I saw Luke coming back with three cups in his hand. He sat down beside me and passed Jake and Mark a drink. Ella gave me a questioning look. "We're seeing who can chug the drinks the fastest. Luke and I tied for first last time, so he wants a rematch," I laughed, looking at Luke.

"Actually," Luke started, "I just want to see who is the ultimate winner, we can't have a tie for first."

"Yeah, whatever," I laughed. Someone started counting down again so I got ready to chug.

"3,2,1, Go!"

I picked up my glass and chugged as fast as I could. I smashed my cup down on the table a good three seconds before anyone else.

"What?!" Mark screamed, surprised at how fast I downed the last one.

"Yes?" I said, trying to keep a straight face.

"How do you keep doing that?"

"Well it's clear to me, that she is no amateur. She's done this before," Jake stated, sounding like a detective.

I bursted out laughing at the three boys as they sat there confused and surprised. Ella, still standing there, joined me and started laughing too. Chris just sat there, looking just as confused as the other boys.

"C'mon Jake," Mark said, getting up from the couch. "We need a game plan so we can beat Julie next time." The two boys left the living room, tripping over their own feet as they went.

"Good luck!" I hollered after them.

"Luck is for losers!" I heard one of them scream back.

"Exactly!" I laughed, standing up to go get some more drinks. As I stood up, I could feel the alcohol hitting. My footing slid and I fell back onto the couch. Luke started laughing like a little girl.

"You are drunk," he smiled, pointing his fingers at me, almost poking me in the eye.

"I could say the same for you," I laughed, attempting to stand again. "Do you want something to drink?"

"I'll have whatever you're having."

"Two coolers, coming up," I smiled, heading to the kitchen.

"Julie!" I heard Mark call, "long time, no see!"

"Mark, it's been like two minutes," I laughed, opening the fridge and grabbing two coolers.

"No, you're lying to me," he said, looking at Jake to see if I was.

"No man, she's right. It's been only two minutes," Jake laughed, taking a swig of Vodka from the bottle.

"Huh. Well, anyway, guess what Julie," Mark said, leaning on the counter for support.

"What?"

"I'm drunk," Mark smiled, as if he'd won an Olympic medal.

I burst out laughing for the second time tonight. "No shit, Sherlock," I said, trying to catch my breath. Jake slipped and fell on the floor which caused Mark to laugh too. Jake just sat on the floor, smiling at his stupidity. Clearly, Jake was gone too. Luke walked into the kitchen and saw all three of us laughing and sat on a bar stool.

"What's so funny?" he asked, noticing Jake on the floor.

"Well, Mark just realized he's drunk and thinks he should win an award," I said, handing Luke his cooler.

"Wait, what? I get an award?" Mark asked, with a sudden excitement in his eyes.

Oh goodness. No, you don't get an award," I laughed, taking a sip from my cooler.

"Well, you don't either," Mark said, pointing his finger at me.

"Awe shucks, that really hurts Mark," I frowned, crossing my arms.

Mark, thinking I was actually sad came up and started poking my shoulder. "Julie, Julie, hey Julie," he said trying to get my attention.

"What?"

"I'm sorry," he said, "you can have my award."

This time Luke started laughing first, "Mark, you don't have an award to give her."

"Oh right," Mark smiled sheepishly, "silly me."

"You guys crack me up," I laughed, walking away to find Ella.

"Toodaloo!" I heard Jake sing from behind me.

"So long!" I called back as I left the kitchen.

CHAPTER 5

I woke up in my bed, my head pounding from last nights party. I sat up and found Ella asleep beside me. I got up as quietly as I could and went upstairs to grab some Advil. Just what I needed, a hangover. I made sure everything was clean because my father was coming home today around three. I grabbed a mug from the cupboard and poured myself some tea.

"Morning," I smiled, when Ella climbed up the steps.

"Good morning, how was your sleep?" she asked.

"I have a killer headache," I admitted. "How did we get home?"

"I drove, you were too hammered to even open the door," she laughed, pouring herself a glass of milk. "I didn't drink anything, so I took us here."

"Thanks," I sighed in relief. The last thing I remembered from last night was leaving the kitchen looking for Ella, "What happened last night?"

"Well . . ." Ella started, taking a seat at the table, "you got pretty drunk from the drinking game you played with Luke, Mark, and Jake. You ended up finding Chris and I, and you told Chris I had a thing for him. And then yo-"

"Oh no. I'm so sorry Ella. I didn't mean to." I felt horrible, what a cow I turned out to be.

"Don't worry about it," she smiled. "Turns out he's liked me for the past two months. So I guess I should thank you."

"Oh, well your welcome, but I still feel awful for doing that."

"It's okay, you didn't do any harm," she said. "Anyway, after that, you found a pool table and ended up playing pool for the next hour. Then you sat on the couch, telling Knock Knock Jokes to anyone who passed. Some of them were actually pretty funny."

"Really?" I laughed.

"Yeah, you're pretty hilarious when you're drunk."

"Well," I sighed, "I guess that's a good thing. Better than being the crazy drunk.

"No kidding," Ella laughed.

"What do you want for breakfast?" I asked, changing the topic.

"A bowl of cereal would be fine."

I grabbed two bowls from the drawer and two spoons as well. I put the cereal boxes on the table and headed back to the fridge for the milk. "I have one question though."

"Hmm?"

"Did Luke and I . . . do anything?" I asked, kind of worried.

"Other than making out the whole night, no," she laughed.

"Oh my God, are you serious?" I asked, shaking now.

"No."

"Ella!" I yelled, relieved that it was a joke.

"What? You were shocked when I said I was a genius," she shrugged. "Pay back is a bitch."

"You almost gave me a heart attack!" I laughed, sitting down and grabbing the Lucky Charms and pouring some in my bowl.

"That's what friends are for," Ella smiled, pouring herself a bowl of Alphabets.

"I'm home," my father's voice rang out as the front door opened.

"Dad?"

"Who else would it be, the mail man?" he said sarcastically.

"You're home early. I thought you were coming back at three?" I asked, clearing the table from our breakfast.

"Well, I caught an earlier flight," my father shrugged, entering the kitchen. "Oh hello," he said when he caught a glimpse of Ella.

"This is Ella," I smiled. "Ella, this is my dad."

"Nice to meet you," Ella smiled, getting up from the table.

"You too," my father said. "I'm going to go take a shower." He left the kitchen and headed upstairs.

I shrugged and Ella and I went downstairs to get changed. I took a quick ten minute shower and re-did my makeup. In the mean time, Ella had re-done her make up as well and changed into clothes.

"You want to go for a walk?" I asked, grabbing my phone.

"Sounds like fun," Ella smiled, getting up from my bed. "Where to?"

"Wherever we end up," I shrugged, jogging up the stairs and out the door, Ella right behind me.

We walked all the way down to the local beach and sat on the sand. We talked for an hour. Ella updated me with the rest of the small details from the party that I couldn't remember. She told me all about her and Chris, and how they may or may not have kissed a few times the previous night. She blushed every time she said Chris' name.

"Awe," I cooed, "you guys would be so cute together."

"Pfft, whatever," she shrugged. "You and Luke were pretty cute last night. He was always at your side."

I blushed, looking at my phone to avoid any eye contact. Just then my ringtone started blaring. I checked the display to see who it was.

"It's Luke," I said, looking at Ella.

"Well, don't just stare at the phone. Answer it!"

"Okay, okay," I laughed. "Don't get your panties in a knot." I hit the talk button and brought the phone to my ear. "Hello?"

"Good morning. How was your sleep?"

"I've got an insane headache, but nothing Advil can't fix," I laughed.

"Same here, I can't remember much after the drinking game we played."

"Me neither. I remember sitting in the kitchen with you and your friends, and then I draw a blank."

"Same story here," he sighed. "So anyways, you want to meet up somewhere?"

"Well, I'm kind of at the beach with Ella at the moment."

"Oh, well I'll call you later then?"

"Yeah, definitely."

"Okay cool, see you later then."

"Okie dokie. See you." I hung up the phone and put it back in my pocket. I looked over at Ella who was staring at me.

Janet VanderMeulen

"What?" I asked, returning the stare.

"Did you just reject Luke?"

"Uh, yeah. Kind of. But I'm already hanging out with you. I'm not going to just leave you and go hang out with him," I said, looking out towards the water.

"Oh yes you are," Ella said. "You will call him back and let him know you're free." I turned and stared at Ella.

"I'll be fine. I am not ditching you for Luke," I sighed, pulling my phone out. "You can hang out with us."

I dialed Luke's number and he picked up on the first ring. "Hello?" he answered.

"Hey, it's me."

"Oh hey! What's up?"

"Ella wants me to tell you that we can hang out right now," I laughed.

"Sweet deal, you want to come over to my place?"

"Yeah, sure. Is it okay if Ella comes along?"

"For sure, Jake and Mark are still here too."

"Alright, we'll be over in twenty minutes."

I hung up the phone and hoisted myself up off the ground.

"Where are we going?" Ella asked, getting up from the ground and shaking off the sand.

"Luke's house," I sighed, walking back towards my house.

We got into my car and I started the ignition. "You sure you want to come?" I asked Ella.

"Absolutely," she beamed, "otherwise you'll be all on your own with those three boys."

I couldn't help but laugh. From what I remembered, those boys were hilarious. They were like brothers to each

56

other too. I figured I would probably see a lot of them around. I shifted into reverse and backed out of my driveway.

Just like last night, we arrived at Luke's in about ten minutes. We walked up the front steps and I rang the door bell.

"Julie!" I heard two boys scream from inside the house, followed by loud footsteps and a thud against the door.

"Hi boys," I laughed as I walked through the door. "You remember Ella?"

"Hey Ella," Jake smiled, shutting the front door.

"LUKE!" Mark shouted at the top of his lungs.

"Ouch, no yelling," I cringed, pointing at my head.

"Hangover? I know the feeling," Jake sighed, leading us to the living room, "not fun."

"I know," I sighed. Just then, Luke walked in the living room and turned off the TV.

"We're going bowling," he announced, ushering us out the door.

"Well aren't you full of surprises," I said, walking back out the front door.

"Sure am," he smiled.

"Shotgun!" Mark yelled, sprinting towards Luke's car.

"Damn," Jake pouted. "You always get shot gun."

"Because you're too slow to call it," Mark said, climbing in the front seat. I got into the back seat and sat in the middle. Jake climbed in on the passenger side and Ella sat on the other side. Luke climbed into the drivers seat and we drove to the Bowling Alley. This was going to be interesting.

"I'm on Ella's team!" Jake yelled, getting out of the back seat.

"I'm on Julie's team!" Luke called, locking his car.

"Well fine then, if that's the way it's going to be. I'm on Mark's team," Mark laughed, walking towards the Bowling Alley.

"Awe, Mark didn't get picked," I laughed, following Mark into the building.

"Whatever, I'll still win," Mark boasted.

We all walked up to the counter and paid for two rounds of bowling. We got our bowling shoes on and headed down to our lanes. We bowled for a good two hours. Ella and Jake ended up winning both rounds. Apparently Ella was pro at bowling. She used to go with her family all the time. Mark ended up joining Luke and I on our team.

We spent most of the time just talking. I found out that Luke had a little sister name Heather. Heather was 15 years old and loved to sing. Luke told me that she was actually pretty good and that I should get her to sing for me sometime. I couldn't meet Luke's family because they had gone on vacation to the mountains for two weeks. They were supposed to be back on Wednesday. Of course, Luke couldn't go again, because his boss wouldn't give him time off of work.

"Well, I better get back home," Ella said, looking at her watch. "My parents will wonder where I am."

"Yeah, me too," Mark said, untying his shoes. We gathered our things and went back to Luke's house.

"I'll drive you home," I said to Ella as I got into my truck. "See you guys around." I waved to the boys and Ella gave me directions to her house.

"Well, that was fun," Ella laughed.

"Yeah, no kidding." I smiled, "very spontaneous." It took us fifteen minutes to get to Ella's house. I dropped her off and waited until she got in the front door before I left. I got home twenty minutes later.

"Dad! I'm home," I called out. No answer. I heard shuffling from the living room and walked over, looking for my father. I turned the corner and a fist flung towards me, knocking me out cold.

*   *   *

The sun had set and it was dark. My body ached from being still for so long. I opened my eyes slightly to find myself laying on the living room floor. I heard my father's heavy snore which told me he was fast asleep. Getting up slowly, I looked around the room. The coffee table was filled with empty beer bottles. He had been drinking. I tip-toed downstairs and went into the bathroom. Turning on the light, I looked at myself in the mirror. I gasped at what I saw. My hand reached up and felt my eye. There was a huge bruise covering my left eye. And there was no way I would be able to cover it up. Not even with my hair. I shut the light off and headed back upstairs. I was starved. I glanced at the kitchen stove. It was 11:15. That means I had been knocked out for at least three hours. I grabbed an apple from the fridge and headed back downstairs to my room. I lay down and thought about what had happened. I thought back to all the days events and came up with two reasons why he had hit me.

1)   I had invited a friend over without him knowing.
2)   I had left without telling him.

Suddenly I felt my phone vibrate in my pocket. I had two unread text messages.

To Julie:
From Ella:
Hey, I think I left my iPod in your truck.

I texted Ella back, even though she was probably asleep.

To Ella:
From Julie:
I'll check in the morning, I didn't get your text till now. Sorry.

I looked at the next message. It was from Carsynn.

To Julie:
From Carsynn:
I have the best news for you! Call me tomorrow, Kay?

To Carsynn:
From Julie:
Sure thing! I'm excited to hear this news :D

I hit send and then plugged my phone in. I changed into my pajamas and plopped back down onto my bed. Within minutes, I was fast asleep.

I woke up, the sun blinding me. Groaning, I got up and looked at the time. It was 11:30. My father had already left for work, so I left my room and went upstairs and had breakfast. Afterwards, I called Carsynn. She picked up within two rings.

"Hello?" she asked, from the other end.

"Carsynn! It's me," I said, heading back downstairs to my room. I looked in the mirror, my bruised eye was even worse than last night.

"Julie!" she screamed. "It is so good to hear your voice. How have you been?" I cringed at the loudness of her voice. My head was still pounding from the unexpected punch.

"Great actually. I have a ton of things to tell you, but first, your amazing news?" I asked, waiting for the awesome news.

"Theoretically, what would you say if my parents told me they were going to pay for a plane ticket for me to come see you?"

"I would say . . . HELL YEAH!" I screamed, despite my headache. "When are you coming?""

"This week."

I sighed. This week was not a good time. I couldn't let her see me with the bruise. She would freak out and I was a terrible liar.

"Julie?" she asked, realizing I had paused. "Everything okay?"

"Yeah, great actually. I'll have to talk to my dad about it. But I'm definitely stoked." I attempted lying anyway.

"What's wrong?" she knew something was up.

"Nothings wrong. Everything is perfect. I guess I'll wait with all my stories until you get here," I said, changing the subject.

"Awe man, c'mon Julie. You know I'm not good with waiting," she whined.

"You can do it Carsynn, I believe in you," I said, encouraging her sarcastically. "When does your plane land in Philadelphia?"

"Friday afternoon. That gives you a whole week to prepare for my awesomeness."

"Alrighty. I'm so stoked. I'll call you tomorrow to let you know what my dad thinks about it," I said, sitting back down on my bed.

"Okay, talk to you soon. And then see you soon after that."

"Yeah, no kidding. That was a nice surprise. Talk to you soon. Bye."

I hung up the phone and sat there, taking everything in. And trying to plan out what I was going to do. First thing, school was tomorrow and I could not show up with a bruised eye. I couldn't lie, especially to Luke and Ella. They would see right through my lies. Second, Luke wanted me to meet his family this week. There was no way I could do that either. Again, not with this bruise. Maybe it would be slightly healed by then. And third, Carsynn was coming to visit. She would instantly know what had happened. She had met my father before. She had told me her first impression of him was that he wasn't that friendly. She would suspect something right away. I would have to come up with some type of story before she arrived. "And the last thing," I sighed, "is my math homework."

I got up and grabbed my textbook from my bag. I sat down at my desk and worked out the math problems, sending my life problems into the back of my mind.

I looked up from my worksheet as my phone went off. "Hello?" I answered.

"I'll be home in an hour and I'm bringing a friend. Make sure you have dinner ready." My father hung up and I just sat there.

"Are you kidding me?" I said out loud. It was 5:00. I had until six to prepare something decent. I went to the kitchen and looked in the pantry. "Spaghetti? I think so," I said, grabbing the noodles from the second shelve.

I got to work right away. I hustled around the kitchen for almost 50 minutes. I quickly set the table and put the last touches on dinner when my father and his friend walked in. He glanced at my face and horror spread across his face. He had forgotten about hitting me. Or he didn't even remember. Either way, he quickly thought of something as the same look spread across his girlfriends face.

"This is Julie, my daughter," he motioned towards me, "and Julie, this is Elizabeth."

"You can call me Lizzy," she smiled.

"Nice to meet you Lizzy," I smiled back politely, something I had done too many times. I walked over to where the two stood and I shook Lizzy's hand.

"And you as well. I've heard a lot about you," she smiled back.

"Perfect," I mumbled under my breath.

"Julie dear, how is your head today?" my father asked, clearly trying to explain my black eye.

"It's better than yesterday," I said, going along with his charade.

"Julie fell down the stairs yesterday morning and she hit her head on the corner of the wall. That's how she got that awful bruise," he said, cringing for effect.

"Oh, that's terrible," Lizzy gasped.

"Clumsy me," I shrugged. "But dinner is ready, we don't want it getting cold."

"Right," my father said. He sat down and gave me a look. I knew the look. It was the 'Get the Hell out of Here' look.

"Uh, I have some homework to finish up on, so I'll just take a plate to my room."

"Okay sweetie, don't work too hard," he laughed.

I grabbed a plate of spaghetti and meat sauce and headed downstairs. Not even a thank you for cooking the damn food. What an asshole.

I fell asleep worrying about the upcoming week. What was I going to tell Luke and Ella? There was no way I would be able to lie to them. I had to think of something, and quick. And how was I going to ask my father if Carsynn could stay at our house.

"Why didn't you tell me?"

I looked up to find Luke standing over top of me. "I couldn't Luke, you have to understand. He would kill me."

"I can't let him keep hurting you," he said, moving towards the doorway.

"Luke, wait! He'll kill you too," I sobbed, reaching for his arm, trying to stop him.

"No. Julie, I love you. And I can't stand by while you get hurt all the time." He left my room and headed upstairs where my father was doing paperwork. Screaming and yelling erupted from the floor above. I tried to get up and help Luke. To try and save him. But my body wouldn't let me. It was like my body was shutting down. Nothing was working except my tear ducts. All I could do was cry, and hope that Luke would be okay. I heard a gun shot and then the sound of a body crashing against the floor.

The next thing I knew, I was standing beside a hole in the ground. I peered into the hole and saw a wooden coffin. I was at someone's funeral. I looked around, trying to find Luke. I didn't see his face anywhere. Instead, I spotted my father, glaring at me. Luke had died; he was trying to save me. This was all my fault.

I woke up covered in sweat and tears. It had been a dream; a really awful nightmare. I looked over at my alarm clock and saw it was only 3:00 am. I tried to go back to sleep but I couldn't. The nightmare kept replaying in my head like a broken record. I couldn't stop it either. I just laid there. What if Luke did find out? What if my father did kill him? A single tear slid down my cheek. How many people would he hurt? More tears began to flow down my cheeks. People were going to get hurt if they found out. My father would stop at nothing to keep everything a secret. The flow of tears began to pour down and I couldn't stop them. I thought about all the problems I was dealing with. It took an hour and a half before I finally fell back asleep, dried tears staining my cheeks.

"Julie! Wake up! You're going to be late for school!" I heard my father call down the stairs.

"I don't feel so good," I called back. I didn't get a reply back. He must have already left for work. That was the plan I had thought of while trying to sleep last night. I wasn't going to go to school until I could somewhat hide this bruise. I would pretend to be really sick until then. That way, I wouldn't have to face anyone and I wouldn't have to meet Luke's family until later. I got up and picked up my cell phone. I called my work, remembering that I had a shift after school.

"Hey, this is Julie. I've caught some kind of flu. I won't be able to come in and work today," I said, clearing my throat for effect.

"Alright dear," I heard Rebecca, my manager, say on the other end, "get better soon."

"Thanks," I said and hung up the phone. I laid back down on my bed and fell back asleep. I had a dreamless sleep. Thank god.

When I woke up next, it was already 12:30. My phone was vibrating like crazy.

To Julie:
From Luke:
Where are you? :(

I sighed as I read the next one.

To Julie:
From Ella:
You okay? Where are you?

I replied back to both messages and told them that I was sick and that I wouldn't be at school today. My stomach growled and I realized I hadn't eaten anything yet. I got upstairs and cooked myself a grilled cheese. I could live off of these things if I was trapped on an island. They were so delicious.

I got another text message.

To Julie:
From Luke:
Awe :(Get better soon!

To Luke:
From Julie:
Thanks :)

To Julie:
From Luke:
Hold on a sec, I'm going to call you.

Sure enough, within thirty seconds I heard the familiar ring.

"Hey there," I whispered, making my voice sound hoarse.

"How are you feeling?" Luke asked.

"I've been better," I laughed quietly. "How was social?"

"Boring as hell," Luke laughed. I heard a lot of talking in the background.

"Are you talking to Julie?" I heard Jake scream in the distance. He must have jogged up because soon enough he had the phone in his hands. "Julie! When are you coming back? I just found out you're in my English class!"

"I'll try and be better for tomorrow," I lied.

"Good, then I won't have to hear Luke worrying about you 24/7."

"Shut up dude," I heard Luke say in the background.

"What? It's true," Jake laughed.

"Well I'm going to let you go and rest. Be at school tomorrow, or I will hunt you down," Jake laughed.

"Okay," I laughed, hanging up the phone. That was something I hadn't thought of. If I was sick for a few days, the boys would come and see me. So would Ella. They would come and keep me company. Dammit. I'd have to find a way to avoid that.

I had a whole day to waste. I decided to take a shower to clean up a bit. I hated looking dirty. It was nasty. I got out of the shower and looked in the mirror again. I gently touched my bruise and cringed. Not only was my eye bruised, but it was swollen. I went upstairs and took an Advil, trying to make the swelling go down a bit. I spent the majority of the next two days lounging around my house.

I got a call each day from Luke and Ella. I kept telling them that my cold was getting worse. They bought it when I would start coughing like a maniac on the other end of the phone line. They would tell me to get better and that would be it. That's how each phone call was. I had told my father about Carsynn's trip here, and surprisingly enough, he told me that it would be fine. He also told me not to breath a word to her about the true reason I had a bruise.

"Well duh, that's a given," I had said to him, rolling my eyes.

"Watch it Julie, or I can arrange for your right eye to match your left," my father threatened.

I scowled at him and left the room, knowing he would stay true to his word. I decided to call Carsynn with the good news.

"Hello?"

"It's a go ahead!" I screamed into the phone.

"Actually?! YES!" she screamed. I could hear her jumping up and down.

"So I'll pick you up at the airport on Friday?" I asked, plopping down on my bed.

"Uh huh. 4:00 in the afternoon," she said.

"Okay, sweet! I am so excited! I have so much to tell you," I said. "But I have to go, so I will see you in two days!"

"Okay," Carsynn laughed. "See you in two days""

"You bet!" I said, "see you then." I hung up the phone and sat on the floor in my room. Carsynn was coming in two days. My bruise would not be gone by then. I had to lie to her. The 'falling down the stairs' story was pretty believable. Carsynn knew I was clumsy. Maybe she wouldn't suspect anything. I hoped she wouldn't.

CHAPTER 6

"Julie! One of your friends came to visit you!" my father yelled down the stairs.

I had drifted off to sleep on my floor, after just laying there for an hour. I sat up quickly and looked at the clock. It was 3:45. School was out and whoever it was must have left once the final bell rang. I bolted for the bathroom and quickly applied some cover up, trying to hide the evidence. Within two minutes, I was walking up the stairs in my pajamas. I was half way up the stairs when I heard Luke's voice drift towards me. Damnit! How did he find my house. I hadn't told him where I lived. Ella must have told him. I reached the top step and I looked towards the kitchen and saw my father sitting on a stool talking to Luke. Luke looked up and saw me. His expression changed from happy to shocked in a split second.

"Hey Julie." He forced a smile, "How are you feeling?"

"Better," I coughed. Luke walked towards me and gave me a big hug.

"I've missed you," he whispered in my ear.

"Let's go downstairs," I whispered back, noticing my father staring at us.

"Okay." We got down to my room and then he was worried again. "What happened to your eye?" He asked.

"I was sleepwalking and I fell down the stairs. I hit the corner and got this," I said as casually as possible. I pointed at the stairs for emphasis, "does it look that bad?"

"It looks like someone punched you in the face," he laughed.

"Great. That's the look I was going for," I joked, leading Luke to one of the couches. It hurt, having to lie to Luke. I wanted to tell him so bad. I wanted to tell him I was being hurt by my father. But I knew I couldn't. After having that dream, I couldn't tell anyone at all. I couldn't risk them getting hurt. That would be selfish. "I have some news for you," I smiled.

Oh? Enlighten me, "Luke smiled, putting his hands together and using a high-pitched voice.

I started to laugh, "I have a friend fr-"

Congratulations," Luke smiled.

"Shut up," I laughed, punching his shoulder.

"Sorry, I couldn't resist."

"Anyway, as I was saying. I have a friend from Seattle and she's coming to visit me."

"Really? That's pretty cool! When does she come?"

"Friday afternoon, at four."

"You still going to hang out with Wittle Wuke?" he asked, putting on his four year old charade.

"Only if Wittle Wuke tells me one thing," I laughed, copying his voice.

"Well, what is it then?" Luke asked.

"When do I get to meet your family?"

I had no idea what Luke thought I was going to ask, but he let out a little sigh of relief. "Whenever you feel better."

"Hopefully it's soon," I smiled.

What Luke did next surprised me. He grabbed my hands in his and looked me straight in the eyes. "Now it's my turn to ask the question."

Oh goodness. Now I know what he was thinking earlier. I let out a little whisper, "yes?"

"You have to be 100% honest with me too."

"Okay." My hands were shaking, I was so nervous. I knew what was coming.

Luke opened his mouth to speak but nothing came out. "Never mind."

"No, what were you going to say?" I asked, curious now.

"It's nothing."

"C'mon, it can't be that bad," I laughed.

All of a sudden, Luke had leaned in and our lips connected. It surprised me. I had not expected this at all. He broke the kiss and we just sat there in silence.

"Well?" he whispered. "Say something."

"That wasn't a question," I whispered, locking lips with Luke once again.

My heart was racing. I had never felt like this before. Yes, I had been with Jonathan for almost a year, but it was nothing like this. This was a completely new feeling.

"I really like you," Luke smiled. "You have no idea."

"Oh, I think I do," I laughed. "How couldn't I? I mean, with the stalking and continuous contact."

"I was just . . . pursuing something great," he smiled. I started blushing. Lucky for me, I had a pound of cover up on to hide it.

"Julie! It's getting late. Say goodbye to your friend," my father called down the stairs.

"His name is Luke!" I called back.

"I don't care what his name is, it's time to say goodbye!"

"He seems like a nice guy," Luke laughed.

"Yeah, he's just a bundle of fun," I said, piling on the sarcasm.

"Well I better go then," Luke sighed, getting up from the couch.

"I guess so." I got up and walked Luke to the front door.

"Get better soon," Luke smiled, pulling me in for a goodbye hug.

"I'll do my best," I smiled, returning the hug.

"See you."

"Bye."

I closed the door behind Luke and turned around to find my father staring at me. "What?" I asked, annoyed that he was always watching me.

"You seem to be pretty cozy with that Luke fellow," he sneered.

"We're just friends, okay?" I made a move for the kitchen to grab some food but my father stood in the way.

"Remember," he whispered, "keep your mouth shut or you can say goodbye to 'Wittle Wuke'"

"You were eavesdropping?!" I screamed, agitated.

"It's my house. I'll do whatever I want," he shrugged.

"You are unbelievable!" I yelled, grabbing an apple from the fridge and heading back downstairs. I needed to do something to clear my mind. I grabbed my iPod from my backpack and turned it on full blast. I drifted off to sleep thinking of Luke, my father, and my mom. God, I missed her.

"I love you and I won't ever leave you," my mom had said.

"I love you too," I sobbed, leaning in to give my mom a hug.

"I won't ever let him hurt you. We'll get out of this soon," she sighed, pulling me in and hugging me. She kissed my forehead to assure me everything would be okay.

"She's gone. She's never coming back," my father said.

"No! She is coming back. She told me she would never leave me!"

"She's dead. She's not coming back. Get that through your thick head," my father yelled at me.

I sat on the floor, balling my eyes out. She had always been there for me. When my father was drinking, she was with me. She would stop him from hurting me. He would never hurt her though. He loved her. He didn't love me. I was a burden. He had told me himself. I realized that she would never be there for me anymore. I would have to take the punches and slaps. I would have to get hurt.

I was in a room that stunk of beer. I was being smashed into the door, over and over again. I looked into my father's eyes and saw nothing. Only hate. The hate I had seen for the past 3 years since she died. Everything blacked out. I was unconscious.

I woke up in Luke's arms. He was smiling at me. He planted a kiss on my forehead. "I love you and I'll never leave you."

"I love you too," I smiled, grabbing his hand.

I woke up drenched in sweat. I began to cry uncontrollably. I didn't want to loose Luke like I had lost my mother. I sat in the fetal position for half an hour, balling my eyes out. By the time I had stopped, it was 3:45 and I couldn't sleep. I tip-toed upstairs and made a grilled cheese. Food was always a comfort thing for me. I ate my food in my room. Then I realized I had forgotten to tell Luke. I grabbed my phone and created a new message.

To Luke:
From Julie:
I really like you too :)

I hit send and finished the rest of my grilled cheese. I crawled into bed and curled up into a ball. I was sleeping by 5:00.

I decided the next morning that I would go to school. Luke had believed my story easy enough. It shouldn't be too hard to convince everyone else. I finished putting my make-up on, still trying to cover my eye, and headed up the stairs. I grabbed a granola bar from the fridge and was out the door by 8:30. I sat in my truck for five minutes when I got to the school. You can do this Julie. When people stare, just smile at them. Luke believed your story, everyone else will too. I opened my door and stepped onto the concrete road. Taking a deep breath, I headed over to the front doors.

I walked in the front doors and kept my eyes on the ground, trying to minimize the amount of eyes looking at me.

"Julie!" Mark yelled, running towards me. Jake and Luke looked up and followed behind Mark at top speed.

Oh god, prepare to be knocked over. Soon enough, I lost my balance in the middle of the group hug the boys had made. Lucky for me, the hug was so tight that I couldn't even fall over if my life depended on it.

"Good to see you Jules," Luke whispered into my ear while Mark and Jake gave each other a high-five.

"Good to see you too," I smiled.

"Julie is in the house!" Jake cheered.

"Man Julie, you must have been one heavy sleeper," Mark said, pointing at my eye.

"Shut up," I laughed, walking towards my locker.

"Julie!" Ella screamed, running towards me.

"Hey Ella," I laughed, when she had finished squeezing me to death in her hug.

"How are you?!"

"You know what," I said, grabbing my English binder. "I feel really great." And that was the truth. I was happy to be back. I had missed Luke and Ella. And Mark and Jake too. They always knew how to make me feel better. They would always be there for me. I made sure that when the time came, I would return the favour.

The morning flew by like there was no tomorrow. Before I knew it, I was sitting in the cafeteria eating lunch with everyone. Luke's friends, Ella's friends, and I had all combined into one group of friends. Everyone knew everyone and mostly everyone got along. I was sitting between Ella and Mark. Luke was sitting across the table with Jake and Chris. Nicole, Jessi, Justin, and Mike all sat on the table to the right. They were the ones that hadn't really adapted to Luke, Mark, and Jake quite yet. They felt that the boys were intruding. I don't know what that was supposed mean. Maybe they were intimidated? Who knows.

"Luke," I said, taking a bite of my sandwich.

"Hmm?"

I swallowed what I had bitten and started to talk," I was thinking, wo-"

"Wow! Julie was thinking!" Mark exclaimed. I punched him in the shoulder, laughing. Mark, Luke, and Jake were so alike. They had the same smart ass comments. But that's why I considered them friends.

"Would tonight be a good night to come over and meet your family?" I asked.

"Awe," Jake cooed, "meet the parents night!"

Luke ignored Jake, "yeah, tonight would be great."

"Great," I said, smiling, "I'll just let my dad know." I pulled out my phone and began texting.

To Dad:
From Julie:
I'll be home late tonight. Catching up on homework at Ella's house.

I sent it and realized Ella had seen the text. She gave me a questioning look. "I'll explain later," I whispered.

She nodded just as the bell rang. "That's my cue," Jake laughed. We all got up and headed to our third block classes, mine being math class. Lovely. I sat down in my regular seat and then I saw Mark enter the class and take a seat.

"Mark," I called out, putting my hand up. He turned around when he heard his name and his face lit up. I motioned for him to come and sit in the chair beside me, which was empty.

"Hey Julie," Mark said, taking the seat, "I didn't know you took math this block."

"Learn something new everyday," I shrugged, settling myself into a more comfortable position. At least this class wouldn't be a complete drag anymore.

Math went by slowly anyway. Mr. Portau decided to surprise us with an in-class assignment. It took most of the period. I finished ten minutes before the bell rang. Because I missed most of the week, Mr. Portau said he wouldn't take it in for marks. It was just for practice.

After class, Mark and I walked towards our lockers together.

"So, you and Luke," Mark nudged my side.

"Why does everyone keep saying that?" I said, putting my hands up in the air.

"Well, I could name a few reasons," he laughed.

"Enlighten me," I said, sarcastically.

"For starters, you hang around him enough that you're now saying the same things," he stated.

"What? No," I said defensively.

"Luke always says 'enlighten me'."

"That's only one thing," I stated.

"Second, you're meeting his family tonight."

"Have you met his parents?" I asked.

"Of course," he laughed.

"So, you and Luke," I laughed, imitating his voice from earlier.

"Okay, okay. Point taken. Friends can meet each others parents," he said, putting his hands up in defeat.

"Thank you," I laughed, reaching my locker.

"But wait, I have a third one," he smiled.

"What?" I sighed, opening my locker.

"You kissed."

I just stood there. "Who told you that?"

"Luke. The boy has been talking about you forever. He was so happy and could not contain his excitement," Mark smirked, leaning against a locker.

"Oh, I see." I sighed. "Well we're just friends."

"With benefits," Mark sang out, so everyone around could hear. I just stood there, with my mouth open, as Mark walked down the hall. I couldn't believe what he just sang. All I could do was laugh because when it came down to it, Mark was right.

"So you're coming to my house tonight?" Ella laughed as I took a seat next to her.

Oh right. I had forgotten about that. "Well, my Dad doesn't like it when I go over to guys' houses. So I just told him I was going to yours. You don't mind, do you?"

"Of course not. Anything to get you and Luke together," she laughed.

"So where's Chris?" I asked, looking around to find his spot empty.

"Doctor's appointment," she pouted.

"Awe buddy." I smiled, patting her back, "so how has it been between you guys?"

"Great!" she piped up. "Perfect, actually."

"You two an item yet?" I laughed, as the bell rang.

"I would've told you," Ella whispered, pulling out her art project.

"Right," I said, taking out my project too. "I have some news for you though."

"Spill."

"I have a friend from Seattle coming to visit me tomorrow," I smiled.

"Really? That's sweet!" Ella smiled.

"And I might have kissed Luke," I whispered, hoping no one had heard it.

"Shut up!" Ella yelled, staring at me.

"Okay," I laughed. I pretended to work hard on my project.

"Scratch that," she said impatiently. "Tell me every little detail." And I did. I told her about everything. The only thing I left out was the bits about my father. "Wow," Ella sighed, "that's something."

"I know," I said, "it surprised me too."

"Oh, I'm not surprised," Ella laughed. "I knew it would happen sometime soon."

"Oh yeah?" I asked, "how?"

"He is always looking at you," she laughed, "and you're always together."

"Hmm," I shrugged, "Mark said the same thing."

"Well Mark knows what he's talking about then."

"I guess so," I sighed. I couldn't help but smile for the class.

"What if they don't like me?" I asked, getting into Luke's car.

"They will, trust me."

"Okay," I laughed, "but it's all on you if they throw things at me."

"What? Throw things at you?" Luke burst out laughing.

"What?" I asked.

"You have one creative mind in there."

"Oh. Well, that's why I'm in art," I beamed.

"Clearly," he said, catching his breath from laughing so hard. We turned onto a new street and Luke's house came into view. I took a deep breath as Luke parked in front of the house.

"Ready?" he asked, looking at me.

"Ready as I'll ever be," I smiled, getting out of the vehicle. I prepared myself for whatever was going to happen when I walked through the door. What would they think of me? Would they ask about my bruise? Would they like me? All these questions had been playing in my head ever since final bell rang.

"Mom, Dad. I'm home," Luke called out as we stepped through the front door.

"Hi Sweetie," his mom called from a different room.

"I have someone I want you to meet," he called out.

Luke's Mom came into view and I was dumfounded. She was so pretty. She looked like she could be a model. She had blonde hair that stopped at her shoulders. She was roughly 5'11 and had sun kissed skin. "Hello," she smiled, walking towards me.

"Mom, this is Julie."

"Nice to meet you," I smiled, shaking her hand.

"And you as well. I've heard a lot about you." I couldn't help but blush. Did Luke talk about me to everyone? My goodness.

"Is Dad home yet?" Luke said, taking his shoes off. I did the same.

"Not yet," Mrs. Hecks said, "he's still at the office. He won't be home until supper time."

"Okay, well we'll be downstairs if you need us," Luke smiled, leading me down the stairs. "There, that wasn't so bad."

"Not really," I said, laughing at my nervousness I had experienced before.

"Luke!" I heard someone yell from upstairs.

"What?" he called back.

"Mom wants to know if your friend is staying for supper."

"Do you want to stay?" Luke asked, turning to me.

"Sure," I smiled.

"Yeah, she is," Luke called back. "And Heather!"

"Yeah?"

"Can you come down here?"

"Yeah, I'll be there in a minute!"

I sat down on one of the couches in Luke's Rec room. There was a pool table, a dart board, and a bunch of gaming systems. Luke came and sat down beside me. He looked back and smiled. "Heather, this is Julie."

Heather came and sat down on the other side of me. "Nice to finally meet you," she smiled.

"You too," I smiled back.

"Do you guys want something to drink?" Heather asked.

"I think I'm good," I sighed.

"Two Cokes," Luke laughed, putting up two fingers.

"Two Cokes, coming right up," Heather smiled, getting up and leaving.

"I like her," I laughed, "she's nice."

"She's my baby sister," Luke shrugged, "what's not to love about her?"

"Awe, you're so cute," I laughed, poking his nose.

"Julie, would you like to be my girlfriend?" Luke blurted out.

"You really know how to make a girl's heart melt," I said after I had recovered from the shock. I had not been expecting him to ask me out. Not like this anyway.

"So," Luke hesitated. "Is that a yes?"

"Absolutely," I smiled, looking into his blue eyes.

He leaned in towards me and I closed my eyes. Our lips met and my heart rate took off. The butterflies awoke in my stomach and took flight.

"Ahem," Heather cleared her throat behind us. We broke apart instantly and my face went beat red. Great.

"Thanks Heather," Luke laughed, taking the Coke's from her hands.

"You're welcome," she smiled, leaving the room again.

"Well that was . . . interesting," I said, moving a piece of hair behind my ears.

"I think I found one thing I don't love about Heather," Luke sighed, opening his can of pop and taking a sip.

I was overcome by emotion when I finally got home that night. I was overjoyed that I was dating Luke. Finally I had someone that I could call my own. On the other hand though, I was really worried. I didn't want Luke to get hurt. I had no idea what to expect in the future. I decided to just go with the flow and see what would happen. I headed down to my room and texted Ella with the good news.

To Ella:
From Julie:
It happened :)

To Julie:
From Ella:
What happened? lol

To Ella:
From Julie:
We're dating :D

To Julie:
From Ella:
You and I, lunch date tomorrow, you're telling me everything
:D

I read the text and started laughing. I was surprised Ella wasn't on her way over to my house right now. Even if it was already 8:30.

I hadn't met Luke's Dad yet. He had to stay late at the office because a client had booked an emergency session. Luke's Dad was a psychiatrist. I thought it was pretty cool. Luke on the other had, did not. His Dad would always know when something was wrong, when something was right. Luke's Dad was always in his face asking how Luke was. Apparently he was like that with everyone. That's just perfect for me.

I headed off to bed around 10:15, knowing that I would have a week and a half with Carsynn starting tomorrow afternoon. We had planned everything out by now. Carsynn would come to school with me and stay with me in my classes. And she would stay at my house while I was at work. She could probably go shopping at the mall or something like that while I was gone too.

CHAPTER 7

I woke up the next morning, more excited than ever. I hadn't seen Carsynn in four years. Today, that would all change. I arrived at school with a big smile plastered across my face.

"Hey Mark, hey Jake," I waved, heading to my locker.

"Hey Julie, still 'just friends'?" Mark laughed, giving Jake a high five.

"Nope," I smiled, passing them and giving them a little push.

"Julie!" Ella called when I rounded the corner.

"Hey Ella!" I called, heading in her direction.

"I am so happy for you," Ella beamed. "I had a dream that this would happen."

"Whoa, wait," I laughed, "you had a dream about me?"

"Shut up," Ella laughed, linking her arm in mine. "You're free at lunch, right?"

"Yeah, I should be. I'll send Luke off with Mark and Jake."

"Good idea," Ella laughed, "we need girl time."

"Yes we do," I sighed as we reached my locker. Someone came up behind me and gave me a hug from behind. "Morning Luke," I smiled.

"Awe, how did you know it was me?" he pouted.

"Who else is going to hug me?" I said. "Plus, your cologne smells amazing."

"You're irresistible. I'm surprised no one else is after you," he smiled.

"Oh shush," I giggled. "There's probably someone out there plotting to get me."

"Don't worry, I'll save you from them," Luke beamed.

"Oh gag me with a spoon," Ella laughed, "at least give me time to leave before you get all mushy."

"One, two, . . ." Luke started. Ella left the scene as fast as possible. "Three!" Luke laughed, planting a kiss on my lips. My stomach did a back flip and the butterflies took off again.

"Way to be Luke!" Jake laughed, slapping Luke on the back.

"Someone always interrupts," Luke muttered under his breath.

"Hey, Ella and I were going to go on a walk at lunch," I smiled, changing the subject.

"Oh, can I come?" Mark asked, sounding like a little kid.

"No," I laughed, "it's strictly, girls only."

"Awe man," Mark frowned.

"Yeah, looks like you're stuck with Luke and Jake," I laughed, grabbing my books.

"Awe man," Mark said, even louder.

"Why are you so upset? She's my girlfriend," Luke laughed, patting Mark on the back.

"I know," Mark smiled, skipping away.

"What a strange kid," I laughed, grabbing my English binder and shutting my locker.

"That's one way to put it," Jake laughed.

I sat down in English class, next to Ella. She tried to get a few details out of me before class started but I wanted to wait to tell her the whole story. She tried to protest, but I stood my ground. She gave up when the bell rang and class started.

"Okay, I think I have waited long enough," Ella stated, sitting down on the grass beside me.

"Well, I went over to his house, and it just happened," I shrugged.

"That's all you have?" Ella asked, exasperated.

"Well, you want all the details?" I asked.

"Uh, yeah," Ella said, "that's why I'm here."

"Fine," I sighed. So I went into a very detailed account of the previous evening. Everything from meeting his Mom to his sister interrupting our kiss.

When I was finished, Ella just sat there staring at me. "I have to meet his sister," she laughed.

"Why?" I said, surprised by the question.

"She seems like a funny gal," Ella laughed.

"Oh, well, I'll introduce you two sometime," I said, smiling. Just then, I caught a glimpse of Luke, Mark, and Jake rounding the corner of the school and sprinting to cover behind another wall. What were they up to? I let it go when I realized Ella was waiting for me to say something.

"Sorry, what?"

"I said," Ella sighed, "what is the name of your friend from Seattle?"

"Oh," I laughed, "Carsynn."

"That's a pretty name."

"I think so too. I'm so excited for you to meet her. You would like her," I said, laying down in the grass and closing my eyes.

"I wouldn't doubt it. Any friend of Julie's is a friend of mine," she said, laying down too.

It was a nice, hot day. I really wished I could jump into my pool at that moment in time. It would be so refreshing. I tried to imagine myself at the pool. I thought back to all those long summer days I had spent sitting on my floaty, tanning. All the days spent alone, without anyone to talk to or confide in. I was happy where my life was headed. I felt comfortable, here in Philadelphia, with my new friends. I was so happy. Everything was finally falling into place and nothing could ruin this feeling.

Or so I thought. I opened my eyes to find a wave of water flying towards me. I tried to dodge it, but failed. Ella, still laying on the ground, oblivious to what had just happened, screamed. Drenched from head to toe, we both looked up to see Luke, Mark, and Jake standing in front of us, buckets in hand.

"Oh, you are so dead," I threatened, getting up from the ground.

"What the hell?" Ella spat. "What was that for?"

"Well, you guys looked pretty hot," Luke started.

"So we decided to cool you down," Jake finished.

"It was for the safety of the public," Mark said, putting his hands up.

"Public safety my ass," I said, lunging towards the guys. They all took off in separate directions. I chased Luke while

Ella tried to catch Mark. Jake was home free . . . for now. I had been in track for several years, one thing I hadn't told Luke. I could tell he was surprised when I caught up to him within thirty seconds. I jumped on his back and tried to take him down to the ground. "You're going to pay," I laughed, attempting to tickle him, hoping he would fall to the ground.

"I'm not ticklish," Luke laughed, "but I wonder..." Luke may not be fast, but he sure is strong. Within one motion, I was off his back and on the ground. He started tickling me from head to toe.

"No fair!" I gasped, trying to squirm out of his grasp, "I'm supposed to get YOU back."

"You're supposed to," Luke laughed, "but I don't see that happening anytime soon."

"That's what you think," I laughed. "You better sleep with one eye open."

"I'm like a dolphin," he smiled.

"What does being a dolphin have to do with anything?" I laughed, curious now.

"Dolphins sleep with one eye open," he said, quite proud of himself.

"Oh," I laughed, "well that was an interesting little fun fact."

"And there's plenty more where that came from," Luke beamed, pulling me up from the ground. Hand in hand, we walked back towards the school.

"Jules, you have to admit, it was funny," Mark laughed, catching up with me after Math.

"It was, but Ella and I plan to get you guys back," I said, looking at him, "and knowing Carsynn, she'll help too."

"Carsynn?" Mark asked.

"Oh jeez. My friend from Seattle," I said, "remember?"

"Oh yeah," Mark laughed, "I remember now."

"I'm picking her up at the airport at four," I beamed.

"O-M-G!" Mark giggled.

I looked at him and just stared, "I'm going to walk away slowly and pretend that never happened."

"It's who I really am!" Mark called after me.

"I'm sure it is," I laughed, grabbing my art things and heading off to class.

"So I've thought of a few things for our revenge," Ella started as I sat down.

"Let's here them," I smiled, having a few ideas of my own.

She opened her mouth to say something but nothing came out. "Okay, I got nothing."

"Don't worry about it," I laughed, "I've got a few ideas on my mind." I started with the worst ideas and ended with the best one. "I think Carsynn would be able to help with the last one," I smiled, seeing the plan form in my head.

"Yes, they are going to feel so stupid," Ella smiled, unpacking her supplies.

"It's perfect," I said, getting up to grab my project from the shelf. My project was almost finished. It was pretty simple, but it had lots of detail. It was a picture of a flower that was just beginning to wilt. Behind the flower were lyrics to my favourite song. The song was about a man who admits he is not perfect and he has made many mistakes. But no matter what happens, he promises that he would always keep trying.

"Julie, your project is coming along nicely," Mrs. Pokis called out, "keep up the good work."

"Thanks," I said, taking my seat again. I grabbed my pen and started working on finishing up the lyrics.

Before I knew it, the final bell had rang and I was sitting in my truck, heading to the airport. I was so excited to see Carsynn. Since the day she called me and told me she was coming for a visit, I had been counting down the days.

I parked my truck in the parking structure and walked in through the main doors. I took a look at the TV's saying when and where the planes were departing and landing. Scanning the screen, I found the one from Seattle. It had already landed. I walked down to the gate where I would meet her at. People were already walking out the doors. Hopefully I hadn't missed Carsynn. She would freak if she found out I was late. I took a seat on one of the benches and waited.

"Julie!" I heard someone call from behind me. I turned my head in the direction the sound came from and saw Carsynn standing there, bags in hand. I got up and ran over to her.

"How did you get over here?" I asked, giving her a giant hug.

Well, I have these things called legs," she started. "I used them to walk over to the luggage belt and grab my luggage."

"Jeez," I laughed, linking my arm in hers, "I have so much to tell you." We walked out the doors I had walked in and headed over to my truck.

"Are you serious?" Carsynn screamed, bouncing in her seat, excited.

"No," I said sarcastically. "I've made all this up for the heck of it." I had just finished telling Carsynn everything that has happened since I moved to Philadelphia. Except for the horrible father part. And as expected, she's been pretty ecstatic about the whole thing.

"When do I get to meet this Luke fellow?" she asked.

91

"Probably tomorrow. Everyone wants to meet you," I smiled, turning into my driveway.

"Nice house," Carsynn gasped, taking it all in. "Since when did you have this much money?"

"My thoughts exactly," I laughed, getting out of the truck. "My dad said he pulled some strings, and I left it at that."

"No use complaining," Carsynn shrugged, grabbing her suitcase from the back.

"Nope," I shrugged, walking in the front door. "Carsynn's here!" I called out.

"Hi Mr. Baxton," Carsynn called out after me.

No answer. "He's probably still at the office."

"Alright," Carsynn squealed, "house to ourselves!"

"Happens more than once," I shrugged, heading down to my room, Carsynn following my lead. "This is my room," I smiled, walking through the door.

"You're living in luxury my friend," Carsynn sighed, falling onto my bed. My phone started vibrating in my pocket.

To Julie:
From Luke:
I'm coming over right now :)

"Uh, Luke says he's coming over right now," I said, reading the text.

"Oh good," she smiled. "I get to meet your knight in shining armour!"

"That's one way to describe him," I laughed.

"Hey Julie," Carsynn said, sitting up on the bed. "What happened to your eye?"

"Oh uh. I may or may not have been sleep walking and I may or may not have fallen down the stairs," I sighed. At least it wasn't a complete lie.

"I could see you doing something like that," Carsynn laughed, falling back onto the bed again.

"Hey now," I said, trying to defend myself.

"Sorry, it's just in your nature," Carsynn laughed, as the door bell rang upstairs.

"Well that was quick," I said. "I'll be right back."

"I'll be here," Carsynn smiled.

I walked up the stairs and headed to the front door. When I opened it, I got a huge surprise. "What are you doing here?" I spat, disgusted by the sight in front of me.

"Julie, I've missed you so much. I want you back."

"How did you find me?" I asked, slightly annoyed.

"I heard Carsynn was coming to visit you, so I followed her here," he said, smiling broadly.

"Well it was a waste of your time. You have to leave," I said coldly.

"But Julie, don't you want me back?"

No," I said, agitated. "I'm with someone else." I started to close the door but he put his foot in the door frame.

"I'm not leaving," he said. "Who's this other guy."

"It doesn't matter Jonathan. Get out of my house."

"I know you love me. You're just too afraid to admit it," Jonathan smiled.

"You cheated on me. How could I ever love you?" I said, trying to shut the door again. No luck.

"Julie, what's going on?" Carsynn asked from downstairs.

"Jonathan's here," I growled, looking back to see Carsynn climbing the last step.

"What the hell man," Carsynn spat. "Get out of here. I told you she doesn't want to see you again."

"I didn't believe you," Jonathan shrugged, keeping his foot in the door.

"You have to leave right now," Carsynn said, advancing towards Jonathan, "or we're calling the cops."

"For what? I haven't done anything illegal."

"Harassment," I stated.

"Harassment my ass," Jonathan said loudly. "I'm just coming to visit my girlfriend."

"I am not your girlfriend anymore. Get that through your head," I said slowly, trying to keep my temper.

"Just leave," Carsynn said, impatient now.

"No," Jonathan said, pushing the door open and walking into the house. I left the front door open and followed Jonathan into the living room. Carsynn was right behind me.

"Julie?" I heard Luke call out from the front door. Oh shit. I had forgotten that Luke was coming to visit.

"Is that your boyfriend?" Jonathan asked, getting up from the couch he just sat down in.

"I'll be right there," I called out to Luke. "Make sure Jonathan stays here," I whispered in Carsynn's ear. She nodded as I went over to where Luke was standing.

"Hey Julie," Luke smiled.

"Hey," I said, "now isn't really the best time."

"Oh," Luke said, his smile disappearing.

"I'm really sorry," I said, feeling horrible for having to send him away.

"Jonathan, stay here," I heard Carsynn say.

"Who's here?" Luke asked, walking towards the living room.

"No on-" I started. I was cut off when Jonathan entered the room.

"So this is your new boyfriend?" Jonathan asked, pointing at Luke.

"Sure am," Luke smiled, putting his arm around my waist. "And who are you?"

"Jonathan, Julie's ex."

"Oh," Luke said, taking a step back. "Nice to meet you?"

"You could say that," Jonathan sneered.

"Jonathan don't," I started. He had that look in his eye. I knew he was going to do something really stupid.

"Don't what? I haven't done anything."

"Don't play dumb with me," I spat.

"I don't know what you mean," Jonathan said, acting innocent.

"If you want me to leave for a bit," Luke said, taking a step back.

"No, you can stay. Jonathan was just leaving," I said, forcing a smile.

"This is news to me," Jonathan said, taking a seat at the table.

I was becoming impatient. This was one of the many reasons why he was called an 'ex'. He was so stubborn. He was completely oblivious to everything around him. He was an overall ass.

"Look man, clearly these girls don't want you hanging around here any longer," Luke stepped in. "Maybe you should leave."

"Hey, I wasn't talking to you," Jonathan said, getting angry.

"Well, I'm talking to you," Luke replied.

"Last time I checked, this is a free country. I can do whatever I want," Jonathan sneered, getting up from his seat.

"Jonathan, get out. I'll call the cops," Carsynn warned.

"They can't do much for you," Jonathan laughed, taking a swing at Luke. Jonathan's hand made contact with Luke's nose and I heard a loud crack.

"Oh my God!" I screamed, running over to where Luke was standing. "Carsynn, call the cops. Call my Dad too!" Carsynn grabbed the phone and ran to the bathroom, locking the door behind her.

"Julie, you don't want to live here. You can come live with me," Jonathan offered.

"Uh no. I like living here, and I sure don't want to live with you," I snapped.

Luke made a sudden movement and next thing I knew, Jonathan was on the floor. Blood was oozing out of his nose too.

"You're going to pay for that!" Jonathan yelled, getting up to his feet and hurling himself at Luke.

"Stop it," I screamed. "Someone's going to get hurt!"

"That someone is Luke," Jonathan laughed.

"The cops are 10 minutes away," Carsynn said as she left the bathroom. She turned the corner and I heard the phone crash to the ground. A look of horror spread across her face as Jonathan crushed Luke against the wall.

"Ten minutes is too long," I said, a tear rolling down my cheek. Without thinking, I pulled out my phone and texted Mark.

To Mark:
From Julie:
Come to my house quick, bring Jake. Luke's in trouble.

I hit send, hoping Luke had told them where I lived. Luke used all his strength to push Jonathan off him and punched Jonathan in the eye.

Five minutes passed before Mark and Jake ran in through the front door. They didn't need any explanation. Jake went up behind Jonathan and pulled his hands behind his back while Mark helped Luke up off the ground. Jake pushed Jonathan against the wall to keep him from escaping.

"Luke," I sighed, rushing over to him, "are you okay?"

"I'm fine," he smiled, sitting down at the kitchen table. I walked over to the freezer and pulled out an ice cube tray. I filled a plastic bag and wrapped it in a cold towel.

"I'm sorry," I said, handing Luke the ice.

"It's not your fault," Luke sighed, cringing when the coldness touched his face.

I heard sirens off in the distance. The cops were here, finally.

"This isn't over!" Jonathan called as the cops came in through the front door. An officer cuffed Jonathan and pushed him out the door. Another officer came into the kitchen and saw all of us.

"What happened?" he asked, pulling out his notebook.

We all took turns talking to the officer alone. I told my side of the story first, from the beginning to the end. After I was done, Carsynn went, and then Luke. Mark and Jake were the last ones to give their statements.

"Well," the officer sighed, "all of your stories match. Mr. Raymond won't be able to contact you guys again."

Thank you," I sighed, showing the officer the door. I caught a glimpse of the clock in the living room. It was already 9:30 and my father wasn't home yet.

"So, I guess you've all met Carsynn," I said, taking a seat at the table. I put my worries to the back of my mind.

"She's a lot like you," Mark laughed, pointing out our similarities. Carsynn looked at me and we both started laughing. So many people have told us that we may be sisters that were separated at birth, even though we don't look alike.

"You guys hungry?" I asked, looking back at everyone else.

"Well my parents are probably wondering where I am," Jake sighed, "so I'll be leaving soon."

"I guess that means I'm leaving soon too," Mark laughed, picking up his keys.

"Thanks for everything guys," I smiled, getting up to show them to the door.

"Anytime," Jake said, "we're always up for an adventure."

"Okay," I laughed. I walked the boys out to their car and said my goodbyes. "How's your nose?" I asked, coming back inside.

"It might be broken," Luke shrugged, "but it'll look bad-ass." I couldn't help but smile. He was so optimistic.

"Do you want something to eat?" I looked over at Carsynn.

"Yeah, I'm somewhat starved," Carsynn said, "airplane food is disgusting."

"No kidding," I laughed, "it's so processed." I scrunched up my face at the thought of the awful food. "Do you want anything, Luke?"

"Nah, I should probably head home too," Luke sighed, getting up from his chair.

"Oh, okay." I walked over to Luke and put my arm around his waist. "Thanks," I whispered.

"Anything for you," Luke smiled. We got out to Luke's car and we stood there for a bit. "No one is ever going to hurt you while I'm around," Luke said after a while.

Except my father, I thought. Luke couldn't protect me from my own flesh and blood. That was impossible without

Luke himself getting hurt. And I wasn't about to let that happen.

"Thanks."

Luke leaned in and kissed my forehead. "See you tomorrow."

"See you," I smiled. Luke got into his car and backed out of the driveway.

"He's so cute," I heard Carsynn squeal from behind me.

"Oh shush," I laughed. "Let's eat."

I couldn't sleep that night. I kept thinking back to what Luke had said. "No one is ever going to hurt you while I'm around." I knew it would hurt him if he found out what my father did. He would do everything in his power to help me. And my father would not be happy if he found out about it. Lost in thought, I finally drifted off to sleep around 3:30 in the morning.

"Julie?" Carsynn asked, shaking me awake.

"Yeah?" I replied, half asleep.

"You were mumbling in your sleep," she said with a worried look on her face.

Oh shit. "What did I say?" I asked, sitting up in bed.

"Something about your father and Luke. You said your father would hurt you more if Luke tried to help," she said, looking me in the eyes.

"Oh," I said. "I guess I say some crazy shit while I'm sleeping."

"Is everything okay?" Carsynn asked, concerned.

"Yeah," I sighed, "why do you ask?"

"I may be blonde, but I'm not oblivious to the world. "You didn't get that bruise from falling down the stairs, did you?" Carsynn asked.

"Yes, I did," I stammered. "I was sleepwalking and I hit my head."

"Julie. You can tell me. I'm your friend."

There was no way I could lie myself out of this. Carsynn always knew when something was wrong. I took a deep breath and began from the beginning.

"To tell you the truth," Carsynn said after I had finished, "I've never really liked your dad."

"Me neither," I laughed between sniffles. Normally, I didn't cry very much. Tonight, I had gone through an entire box of tissues.

"I don't blame you," Carsynn sighed. "Does Luke know?"

"No," I said, another tear rolling down my cheek. "If I tell him, he'll do everything to get me out of here. My father will be so angry and probably hurt Luke in one form or another."

"Oh Julie, we have to help though. We can't just sit here while you get hurt."

"You have to. If my father finds out that anyone knows, I will be in so much trouble. More than I am right now."

"I'm so sorry," Carsynn said, pulling me into a hug. We had been talking for an hour and I was wiped out. My eyes were stinging from all the crying I had been doing.

"I'm tired," I yawned. "Can we talk more tomorrow?"

"Yeah, sure," Carsynn said, settling back into bed. "Goodnight Jules."

"Good night," I said, turning off the light. "And thanks."

"Anytime Hun."

CHAPTER 8

I woke up at 11:30, thanking the Lord it was Saturday. With all the crying I had been doing last night, my eyes were all puffed up. I got up as quietly as I could and headed to the bathroom to take a shower. I was so tired. Last night, Carsynn had found out about everything. She knew my father was a self absorbed drunk who could care less if he knocked me out cold. She knew my deepest secret that no one else knew. I needed to make sure she was the only one that knew. Anyone else would make the situation that much worse; I could trust Carsynn.

I hopped out of the shower and headed upstairs. I decided to cook up some french toast; I knew it was Carsynn's favourite breakfast food.

"Smells delicious," Carsynn yawned, appearing at the top of the steps. "French toast!" she squealed, pulling up a chair. "My favourite!"

"I know," I laughed, bringing the food to the table and sitting down.

"You're the best," Carsynn said through a mouthful of french toast.

"I know." I poured two glasses of milk and began to plan out the day, "Today was supposed to be the day that you met everyone, but since you've already done we'll just go and hang out with everyone," I laughed.

"Sounds like a plan to me," Carsynn smiled.

"We're all going out for supper around 4 o'clock. Sound good?"

"Yes ma'am." Carsynn finished up with her breakfast and cleared both our plates.

"Hey Carsynn?" I asked, getting up from the table.

"Hmm?"

"About last night," I started.

"Yeah?" Carsynn replied, looking up.

"Could we keep this between us?"

"Sure thing," Carsynn smiled, coming over to me and pulling me into a hug. "What are best friends for?"

We spent most of the afternoon gossiping about people back in Seattle, since Carsynn didn't know anything about anyone here. Of course, that would soon change. Before we knew it, it was already 3:45. We had been getting ready for the past hour, so we headed out the door, ready for an evening of fun.

"So we meet again," Mark laughed, nodding at Carsynn and I.

"Yes we do. Jake right?" Carsynn asked, pointing at Mark.

"Mark," he laughed, "that's Jake." Mark pointed over at Jake who was walking up towards the diner. We decided to eat at Johnny Rockets; the food was always amazing.

"My bad," Carsynn laughed, looking over at Jake.

"I think everyone is here except for Ella and Chris but they couldn't make it," I said, looking at my watch.

"Let's eat!" Luke yelled, herding everyone into the diner.

By the time we finished eating and got out of there, it was 7 o'clock.

"I vote we all come back to Julie's place," Carsynn shouted, "shotgun!" Before anyone could protest, Carsynn was in my truck, beckoning everyone else over.

I couldn't help but laugh. "Carsynn, you automatically get whichever seat in the truck, you're the only passenger."

"Just letting the world know that I called it," Carsynn smiled, motioning for the boys to get in their vehicle.

"Well, I guess it's been decided for us, we're all going back to your place," Luke laughed, heading over to his vehicle. Mark and Jake followed suit and got into Luke's car as well. I hopped into my truck and we headed back to my place.

I pulled into the driveway, got out of the truck, and headed over to the front door to unlock it.

"I think the boys got lost," Carsynn laughed, dropping her bag on the counter.

"They probably took the long way here," I sighed, pouring a glass of water for the both of us.

"Who knows," Carsynn shrugged, sitting down on a stool.

The boys walked in the front door 15 minutes later, arms full of alcohol.

"Of course," I laughed as the boys walked in. "You would stop and get booze."

"Woo! What did you get?" Carsynn smiled, turning her stool around to face the boys.

"Whatever we could get, it's hard finding someone to buy alcohol at this time of day," Marked said sarcastically, grabbing a beer for himself.

"Time to get crazy," Jake laughed, grabbing the bottle of vodka and pouring himself a shot.

"You guys are lucky my dad isn't home," I sighed, grabbing a cooler out of the bag."

"Correction, your dad's lucky he's not here," Mark laughed, "otherwise he'd have to deal with a bunch of out of control teenagers."

"Yeah, what Mark said," Jake said.

"You guys are idiots," I laughed. "He would get you out of the house faster than you could say 'party'."

"I could take him," Luke said, puffing up his chest.

"In your dreams," I said, winking at him.

"Ouch," I heard Carsynn say from somewhere to the left.

I struggled to open my eyes, but when I did, I found myself lying on the floor in my basement. "What the hell?"

"Some night," Carsynn sighed, getting up from the couch and heading to the bathroom.

"That's one way to put it," I said, getting up from the floor. That's when I saw that all the boys were still here. Mark and Jake were sleeping on the other two couches and Luke was sleeping on the floor two feet from where I was. Definitely a good thing my father was not around this morning. I tip-toed upstairs to start making some breakfast. Looking at the time on the stove, I guessed the boys would be starved. It was almost one in the afternoon. I checked my phone to see if there were any new messages.

To Julie:
From Dad:
I'll be home around 7. Make sure dinner's ready.

Well, at least that gave me plenty of time to clean up the house.

"I'm thinking a huge amount of bacon and eggs will fill their stomachs," Carsynn smiled, appearing at the top of the stairs.

"I'm sure the smell of that will wake them up too," I laughed, grabbing two frying pans from the cupboard. "Bacon or eggs?"

"I'll cook the eggs," Carsynn said, "the bacon grease always burns me."

"Alright, I'll risk my life this morning," I laughed, grabbing the ingredients we needed to cook. Carsynn grabbed a frying pan and started cracking eggs into a bowl.

"The boys better be satisfied with this," Carsynn said, turning the burner on.

"I'm sure they will." I opened up the bacon and dropped some slices into the frying pan. "So my dad gets home at seven," I said, changing the topic.

"Well," Carsynn sighed, looking around. "We better get this place cleaned up before then."

"Ain't that the truth," I sighed, setting the table for five.

"Good morning beautiful," Luke yawned as he reached the top of the stairs.

"Awe, thanks," Carsynn smiled, putting the food on the table.

"And good morning to you too Carsynn," Luke sighed, as he walked over to me and planted a kiss on my cheek.

"Are the other two up yet?" Carsynn asked, heading towards the staircase.

"Not one bit," Luke laughed, sitting down at the table.

"Well, I can change that." Without another word, Carsynn was down the stairs. A moment later I could hear her screaming. "Get up you sleepy heads. Breakfast is served!"

"Don't talk so loud," I heard one of the boys say, half asleep.

"Don't drink so much," Carsynn joked. She ran up the stairs and joined us at the table, "they're up."

"I don't doubt that statement one bit," I laughed.

"I love bacon," Jake sighed, reaching the top of the stairs.

"That is good to hear," I smiled, "there's a lot of it to go around."

"Hardly enough for Jake here," Luke joked, helping himself to some eggs.

"I'll get by," Jake laughed.

"Whoa, whoa, whoa," Mark said, finally upstairs. "Save some for me!"

"Should've gotten up earlier," Jake shrugged.

"I was up before you!" Mark protested.

"Correction, you were awake before me," Jake pointed out.

"Whatever, pass me the bacon," Mark said, taking a seat.

"You snooze, you lose."

"Screw you Jake," Mark laughed, grabbing the plate himself.

"Well aren't you two cute," Carsynn sighed. "You're like a married couple. Why not make it official?"

"You're so funny," Jake said sarcastically, sticking his tongue out.

I loved my new friends. Of course, I love Carsynn as well. I wish Carysnn lived in Philadelphia; life would be that much more bearable. I got up from the table and started to collect all the empty bottles and cans laying around the kitchen.

"So, who remembers what happened last night?" Jake looked around the table for an answer; nothing but silence.

"Well clearly it was a great night then," Mark joked, clearing everyone's plates from the table. "I mean, by the looks of this place and the size of my headache, it had to have been a great night. There's no doubt about that one."

"It was definitely a night well spent," Jake smiled. "I would love to stay and help clean up, but I have to work at three. Thanks for breakfast though!"

"You are very welcome," I smiled, taking a seat on the stool.

"Well, that means I'm headed home to then," Mark sighed, "unless you want to give me a ride Luke."

"You know I love you buddy," Luke laughed, "but you don't live anywhere near me."

"That's what I thought," Mark said, laughed. "Later guys."

"See you later boys," Carsynn said, waving goodbye.

"Adios amigos," Jake said, closing the front door behind him.

"I wish I could stay too," Luke sighed, getting up from his chair, "but my mom texted me this morning. Apparently its pretty disastrous at our house too."

"It's fine," I laughed, "I have Carsynn as my own personal slave."

"Oh I must have forgotten," Carsynn piped up, "I have some-"

"-where to be?" I laughed, "yeah, okay then Carsynn."

"At least I tried," she shrugged, picking an empty chip bag up from the floor.

"Good luck," Luke laughed. "Later hun, I'll see you tomorrow." I walked over to him and gave him a quick peck on his lips.

"See you tomorrow," I smiled.

Just as Luke closed the door, Carsynn squealed, "oh, you two are so cute!"

"Oh shush,' I laughed. "Let's get to work."

We spent the next two hours cleaning the entire house. By the time we were finished, it was almost four o'clock. We were so tired out from the night before so we decided to take a quick power nap before my father got home from his trip. As soon as my head the pillow, I was fast asleep.

CHAPTER 9

My head shot up off my pillow; my eyes immediately darting towards my alarm clock. I saw the time and realized we had overslept. It was already eight thirty which meant my father was already home.

I looked over to see Carsynn fast asleep beside me. I got out of bed as quietly as I could and tip-toed upstairs. "Dad?"

Of course, there was no reply as usual. Instead, I just followed the sounds of the TV to the living room. As I entered the room, my father got up off the couch.

"Where did you stay last night?" I asked, looking around for any empty bottles of whiskey; not a single one.

"It doesn't matter where I stayed," he scowled. "You don't have to know my whereabouts 24/7."

"Sorry, I was just curious," I sighed, taking a seat on the couch.

"I thought I told you to have supper ready," my father said, a glare spreading across his face.

At that moment, I wished I would have been anywhere else but there. A lump began to form in my throat as I tried to think of an excuse; nothing. "I am so sorry. I completely forgot. I fell asleep and be-"

"I don't want to hear it!" my father shouted.

All I could do was just sit there and let him get the anger out of his system.

"I ask you to do one simple thing," he yelled, "and of course, you can't do that."

"Dad, Carsynn's downstairs," I whispered, hoping he would quiet down.

"It's my house! I say what I want when I want," he said, still at a very loud volume. "You never cease to disappoint me!"

"I'm sorry," I whispered.

"Shut up!" he yelled. And just like that, he was lunging towards me. I tried to get out of the way, but he was too quick for me; he was definitely sober. "You're a sad excuse for a daughter," he yelled as his fist collided with my left shoulder.

I cringed as the pain spread throughout my arm; a tear rolled silently down my cheek.

"Get out of my sight!"

I got up from the couch as fast as I could and ran upstairs, not giving him another chance to strike. I ran into the bathroom and locked myself in. My chest started heaving up and down as the sobs struggled to escape. I rolled up my sleeve to observe what damage had been done this time. That simple gesture sent pain shooting up and down my arm; it was unbearable. I turned towards the mirror and looked at my shoulder. It was already bruising where his knuckles had connected with my body. Even the smallest movements were almost impossible. More tears started rolling down my cheeks; my shoulder was starting to swell.

"Julie?" I could hear Carsynn whisper from the other side of the locked door.

"Yeah?" I asked, wiping the tears away with my right hand.

"Can I come in?"

"I'll be right out," I sighed as I rolled down my sleeve.

I unlocked the door to a very worried Carsynn. "What happened?"

I couldn't put on the tough girl act this time. "It hurts so much," I cried, cradling my arm to minimize movement.

"C'mon," Carsynn said. "I'll drive."

We got to the hospital about quarter after nine. Before we got to see the doctor, it was almost ten o'clock.

"Julie Baxton," the nurse had said.

"I'll be right here," Carsynn said, motioning me towards the the nurse. I nodded my head and headed towards the white curtains.

"So what happened here?" The doctor asked as I took a seat on the bed. He rolled up my sleeve and took a look at my shoulder.

"I, uh, fell down the stairs," I lied, cringing in pain.

"That must have been quite the fall," the doctor joked, pressing my shoulder lightly.

"Yeah, sure was," I said, trying to move away from the pain.

"Sorry about that. We'll have to do some x-rays to see if there are any broken bones." The doctor got up and I followed him out the room to Radiology.

"It looks like you fractured your clavicle," the doctor said, pushing back the curtains. "You're going to have to wear a sling around your arm until it fully heals. You don't want it to heal in the wrong place. That will just bring you a world of pain."

"Sounds exciting," I said sarcastically, despite the situation. The doctor grabbed a sling from the cupboard and helped me get my arm into it. "Thanks Doctor," I smiled as I walked out of the room and back to the waiting room.

"So?" Carsynn asked, getting up from her chair.

"I have a fractured shoulder," I sighed, motioning towards the exit with my free arm.

"How long are you in the sling for?"

"Two whole weeks," I groaned.

"I'm so sorry Jules," Carsynn said, opening the truck door for me.

"It's not your fault," I said. "It's mine."

"It is not your fault Julie," Carsynn started. "There is no reason that any hum-"

"Can we just forget about it?" I asked, leaning against the window.

"Julie!" Carsynn exclaimed, "you can't just brush things like this off. You have to deal with it otherwise it will never go away."

I couldn't even muster up a response. My mind was focussed on the pain I was in. We got back to my house and we retreated to my bedroom. I tried laying down with much difficulty; not one single position was comfortable, obviously. I ended up propping myself up with a pillow and trying to sleep that way.

"Jules?" Carsynn whispered.

"Yeah?"

"Why'd he do it?"

"I forgot to make him supper."

Carsynn did not even reply to the last comment. It was on that note that I finally fell asleep around eleven thirty.

My alarm clock rang at 7:00 o'clock sharp. "Do I have to get up?" I moaned in pain.

Carsynn mumbled beside me.

"Get up," I sighed, rubbing my eyes. "School."

"Oh man," she groaned, sitting up in bed. "How's your shoulder?"

"Never felt better," I said sarcastically, getting out of bed. "If you need a shower, you can use the ones upstairs."

"Will do," Carsynn smiled, trying to lighten the mood.

I took my sling off and tried to take a shower. It was hard to wash my hair, but I got it done eventually. When I got out of the shower, I found Carsynn upstairs, grabbing a bowl of cereal.

"Carsynn?" I asked, grabbing myself a bowl.

"Yeah?"

"Do you want to know exactly what happened last night?" I asked, sitting at the table.

"Only if you want me too," Carsynn replied, joining.

"You deserve to know," I said, managing a weak smile. I started the story from the moment I woke up to the moment Carsynn found me in the bathroom. After I was finished, Carsynn was in utter shock.

"That is not even fair!" Carsynn yelled, slamming her fist on the table.

"Shh," I whispered. "My dad might still be here. I don't know if he works today."

"Sorry," Carsynn said, lowering her voice. "That is not even fair."

"You're telling me," I laughed.

"It's not funny Julie," Carsynn frowned, "I mean, look at you. He fractured your-" she paused. "Your whatever you call it."

"Clavicle?" I asked.

"Yeah, that thing. That isn't nothing Jules."

"I know, I know," I sighed, finishing up my bowl of cereal.

"What are you going to tell everyone at school?"

"Well, I was thinking. We could say that I hurt it the night before when we all got drunk," I said. "I just didn't realize it until later when it started getting sore."

"Meh, it's believable enough," Carsynn shrugged. "As long as no one looks up clavicle injuries and realizes you feel pain instantly."

"Let's just hope they don't," I laughed.

We got to school just before the first bell rang. This left us with no time to hang out with anyone. Personally, I had no problem with that.

"What the hell happened to you?" Jake said loudly, getting up immediately.

"Mr. Johnson," Mrs. Doril piped up. "Watch your language!"

"Sorry Mrs. Doril," Jake sighed, turning back towards me. "Well?"

"Turns out I hurt my shoulder Saturday night," I shrugged, laughing for effect.

"Is that so?" Jake asked, eyes narrowing.

"My shoulder started aching after you all left so Carsynn drove me to the hospital," I said, taking a seat.

"She'll have this bad boy for two weeks," Carsynn laughed, pointing at my sling.

"Lucky you," Jake said, sitting back down.

"Where do I sit?" Carsynn asked, looking around.

"Good question," I laughed. "Just a second." I got up from my seat and went to talk to Mrs. Doril. "I have a friend from Seattle who is staying with me for the next week. Is it okay if she comes to class with me?"

"Of course," Mrs. Doril smiled, "what's your friend's name?"

"Carsynn," I said.

"Well Carsynn can just pull up a chair beside your desk." Mrs. Doril motioned towards a stack of chairs at the back of the room. "But don't get distracted, otherwise Carsynn will not be able to sit in anymore."

"Deal," I smiled, heading back to my seat. Ella walked in just as the bell rang and rushed to her seat.

"What did you do to yourself?" Ella asked, noticing the sling.

"I may or may not have fractured my shoulder."

"How?"

"I don't remember," I laughed, changing the subject. "This is Carsynn, by the way."

"Hey," Carsynn smiled, sitting down.

"Nice to meet you Carsynn," Ella smiled. "I'm Ella."

"It's nice to meet you too," Carsynn laughed. Mrs. Doril made her way to the front of the room as class began. Turns out we were starting a novel study today; a play by Shakespeare. Mrs. Doril went over the projects we were supposed to complete during the first act. After that, we all got into our own groups. Of course, Jake, Carsynn, Ella, and myself were in a group together.

"How convenient," Carsynn laughed.

"What's that?" I asked, grabbing my play book.

"I get to join you in class when it's interesting rather than when you're writing something like an essay."

"That is convenient indeed," Jake said in a British accent. Ella, Carsynn, and I all looked at each before we all bursted out laughing.

"What?" Jake asked, confused.

"Nothing," Ella laughed, taking a deep breath. "Let's do this."

"Well, alright then," Carsynn smiled. "Dibs reading the King's lines."

"What? No way!" Jake cried. "I'm the dude in the group. It only makes sense that I read the King's lines."

"Over my dead body," Carsynn said, picking up the book.

"Rock, paper, scissors," Jake said, putting his hand in a fist.

"Fine," Carsynn sighed. "Rock. Paper. Scissors!"

"Oh, come on!" Jake yelled, getting defeated by Carsynn's paper. "Best out of three!"

"Nope," Carsynn laughed, "I won fair and square."

"I hate this," Jake grumbled. "I quit."

"You can't quit," I laughed.

"Thank you Captain Obvious," Jake said sarcastically.

"Is someone a little grumpy?" Ella asked. "Cheer up buttercup."

"Fine," Jake sighed, "I dibs the cool sidekick, whoever that is."

"He's all yours," Carsynn laughed.

"You shush," Jake laughed, picking up his book.

"By the way, you, Carsynn, and I are going for a walk," I said, looking at Ella.

"But no interrupting boys this time," Ella said, rolling her eyes at Jake.

"Huh? I don't know what you're talking about," Jake said, pretending to begin reading.

"I bet you don't," Ella laughed.

For the rest of the class, I kept thinking about what I was going to say to Luke. I mean, I knew what I was going to say. It was just a matter of how I was going to say it and whether or not he would believe my story. I dreaded the end of the period, knowing I'd have to face him sooner or later. Of course, the class went by quickly and I was walking through the hallways before I knew it.

"Hey hon-" Luke started saying before looking down at my sling. "What happened?" he asked, suddenly worried.

"Well," I said taking a deep breath.

"Turns out she hurt her shoulder Saturday night," Carsynn laughed, "she's accident prone." I was so glad Carsynn was here. No matter what, she always had my back.

"I've noticed," Luke sighed. "Are you okay?"

"I've been better," I laughed, "but I'll be fine."

"I'm so sorry," Luke said, looking directly at me.

"It's not your fault," I sighed, trying to hug him in a way that didn't hurt.

"Yes, it is." Luke sighed, "C'mon, let's get to class." He grabbed my books and we all walked to class together.

I felt so terrible lying to Luke. Of course, there was no way around it. I had to lie to him for obvious reasons.

"It'll be okay," Carsynn whispered in my ear.

"Thanks," I smiled, taking my seat in the back. Carsynn pulled up a chair just like she did in English. Mr. Culter had given us the go ahead too.

About half way through class, Mr. Culter moved Luke to the front of the room. Apparently he was distracting everyone around him.

"I have done no such thing," Luke defended, when Mr. Culter had accused him.

"Well not everyone," Mr. Culter sighed, "just Ms. Baxton." I blushed and slouched down in my chair.

"If anything, she was distracting me," Luke laughed, taking his seat in the front.

"It doesn't matter," Mr. Culter said, "you're sitting here for the next week."

"Perfect," Luke said sarcastically. "Now I can distract someone else."

"You will do no such thing," Mr. Culter said sternly.

"So, what does this walk entitle?" Ella asked, approaching Luke, Carsynn, and I at my locker.

"Walk?" Luke asked, eyebrow raised.

"Don't you worry your pretty little head about it," Carsynn laughed.

"Pretty little head?" Luke said, confused.

"See you later," I laughed, giving Luke a goodbye kiss. We pushed through the cafeteria doors and headed for a grassy area to sit.

"Well, we had a bit of a surprise Friday night." I started filling Ella in on everything she had missed. I told her all about Jonathan's visit. I told her how Luke had come just after and they began to fight. Carsynn told her all about the cops taking Jonathan away.

"Holy cow," Ella said after we finished, clearly stunned.

"I know," Carsynn laughed, "talk about first impressions."

"Yeah, that was one crazy first night," I admitted.

"You can say that again," Ella laughed, "I wasn't even there and I think it's pretty intense."

"Oh, one thing I forgot to tell you," I said, turning to Carsynn. "Friday, the boys thought it would be funny to dump water all over us. So we've come up with a plan to get them back."

"Oh good. I love revenge plans," Carsynn laughed, rubbing her hands together.

"Good," Ella smiled, "we're going to need your help."

"Count me in," Carsynn laughed.

My boss sent me home early that day. She told me that I didn't have to show up to work as long as my shoulder was fractured. Once the sling was off, she would let me come back to work. Of course, I couldn't complain. I headed home to change into some fresh clothes. Carsynn had gone home with Ella so she wouldn't be bored at my house.

"Julie," my father called out when I walked through the front door.

"Yeah?" I sighed, dropping my bag on the floor.

"Come hear, I need to talk to you."

"About?" I asked, opening the refrigerator.

"Just get in here," he yelled.

"I coming," I said, annoyed. I caught a glimpse of an empty vodka bottle sitting on the counter. My heart sunk in my chest.

I walked into the living room and sat on the opposite side of the couch, crossing my legs. "Yes?"

My father took a look at my sling before continuing, "you and this Luke fellow. Are you two close?"

"Yeah, we're uh . . ." I stopped mid-sentence. Should I tell him? He had no reason to be upset about it.

"You're what?" my father asked impatiently.

"We're dating," I muttered.

"Oh really," my father laughed.

"What's so funny about it?" I asked, shocked at his reaction.

"Nothing, but remember. Keep your home life out of it," he warned.

"As in, don't tell him you beat me for fun?" I spat.

"You think you'd learn to keep your attitude under control after all this time," my father sighed, getting up from the couch. I braced myself for what was to come. To my surprise, he walked passed me to the kitchen. "You're lucky I messed up your shoulder yesterday. Otherwise you would have gotten another lesson today."

CHAPTER 10

"Oh hello Julie," Ella's mom smiled, opening the front door. "How's your arm?"

"It's alright," I sighed, thankful that Ella or Carsynn had already explained for me. "How are you?"

"I'm great. Come inside," Ms. Reid smiled. Ella's mom was and has been single ever since Ella turned eleven. Her husband walked out on them and moved to New York, to be with a woman he had been seeing regularly during business trips. "Ella and Carsynn are downstairs."

"Thanks," I smiled, heading down the stairs.

"Jules!" Carsynn screamed, jumping from the bed when I entered the room.

"Hey," I laughed, plopping down on the corner of the bed. "Having fun?"

"Plenty," Ella laughed, grabbing her camera and handing it to me. I turned it on and flipped through all the pictures.

"Nice," I laughed, looking at a picture of Ella and Carsynn attempting hand stands in the back yard.

"So Ella and I were thinking," Carsynn started. "We should go out and watch a movie tonight."

"Which movie is playing?" I asked.

"They're playing a movie called Enough at the drive-in theatre," Ella smiled.

"What's it about?"

"No idea," Ella laughed, "but I do know Jennifer Lopez stars in it."

"Well, consider me in," Carsynn said, "let's head out!"

We all got into my truck and Carsynn drove us over to the drive-in theatre. The lot was practically empty, with the exception of a few vehicles.

"Well, I want some popcorn," Ella said, getting out of the vehicle.

"Hurry up," I called after her. "The movie is starting." Ella started jogging over to the concession to beat a family also headed in the same direction.

"One large popcorn and three medium cokes please," Ella said, pulling out her wallet.

"Sure thing," the cashier smiled, putting the order together.

"Okay, so here's the plan," Ella said, getting back in the truck. "We'll share the popcorn and drink our own drinks."

"Well, that sounds like a great plan indeed," Carsynn said in a British accent. I thought back to English class and started laughing.

"Ha. Ha." Ella rolled her eyes as she passed out the refreshments.

"Stop your bickering, the movie is starting," I laughed, grabbing some popcorn and shoving it in my mouth.

"Hungry much?" Carsynn laughed, grabbing some popcorn too.

"Shut up, I didn't have any supper," I laughed, grabbing another handful.

The movie began and we all settled into our seats. As the movie progressed, I felt an all too familiar feeling that I did not want to feel. Turns out, the movie was about a young woman who married an abusive man. She decides to run away from her husband with her daughter Gracie, but he ends up finding her. No matter what the woman does, the man always finds her.

I could sense Carsynn looking over at me a number of times, but I always faced forward, pretending to focus on the screen. But I did not watch the movie; I couldn't stop thinking about Luke. I had always thought that one day, I would be able to runaway from my father and never be hurt again. Truth was, he would always find me; there was no way I could escape his grasp.

"Can we go home?" I asked, wanting to be anywhere but here.

"Is everything okay?" Ella asked, taking her eyes off the screen.

"I just don't feel that great," I said, suddenly feeling faint.

"Oh, well of course we can go home," Carsynn said, knowing the real reason why I wanted to leave.

"Yeah, sure," Ella smiled. "This movie kind of sucks anyways."

"You can say that again," Carsynn said. Carsynn put the truck into reverse and headed back towards Ella's house.

"I hope you feel better," Ella said as she stepped out of the truck. She waved goodbye as she walked towards her house. She went inside and shut the front door behind her.

"I am so sorry," Carsynn said, turning towards me.

"It's alright, you had no idea," I said, looking out the window.

"Are you okay?"

"Yeah, I'll be fine," I lied.

"Are you sure?" Carsynn started the ignition and pulled out of the driveway.

"Yeah, don't worry about it. I just couldn't stand the movie any longer."

"Julie, you can talk to me, you know that," Carsynn said, turning to look at me.

"Yeah, I know, it's just-" I hesitated, not knowing if I should go further.

"It's just what?" Carsynn asked, persistent to find out what was bothering me.

"It's just that I don't know what to do about Luke," I blurted out.

"What do you mean? You like him, don't you?"

"Well yeah, but I just don't think I'm being fair to him."

"You just need to tell him the truth," Carsynn said softly.

"I can't!" I cried.

"Yes you can," Carsynn urged. "You just need to find the courage to do it."

"If I tell him, someone's going to get hurt," I said, not changing my mind.

"Someone's already getting hurt," Carsynn cried.

"Well better me than anyone else," I sighed.

"Don't say that. No one deserves to be treated like this, no one," Carsynn said, pulling into my driveway.

I didn't know what to say to her after that. Clearly she was determined to get me out of this situation. I was grateful that she was trying, but it just simply wasn't going to work. My father would freak out and start hurting the people around me. I just had to deal with it, on my own. I knew exactly what I needed to do.

*   *   *

"So that's the plan, is it?" Carsynn laughed, looking at her watch.

"You bet, do you think you can handle it?" Ella asked.

"Oh, don't you worry. Those boys will be done like dinner," Carsynn laughed, rubbing her hands together like an evil villain.

"I am so excited, aren't you?" Ella asked, looking at me.

"Huh?" I looked up at Ella. "Oh right, yeah. Definitely."

"What's been up with you lately?" Ella asked, looking worried.

"I haven't been feeling too great," I lied, getting up from my seat. I could see Luke, Mark, and Jake crossing the lawn and coming towards us. Before they got any closer, I made an excuse that I had some homework to catch up on and fled the seen.

"Where's Julie going?" I heard Luke ask as I disappeared into the school.

I found an empty table in the library and took a seat. I didn't actually have any homework to catch up on, which left me to just sit there and think. So far, I'd been sticking to the plan. For the past few days, I've been putting a bit of distance between myself and Luke.

We've haven't hung out with each other outside of class. Eventually he would get tired of me and move on to someone else.

"Hey you."

I looked up to find Luke taking a seat across the table. "Hey," I sighed, looking down at the table. Clearly it was going to take some time.

"Ella told me you had some homework to catch up on," Luke said, looking around, not finding any homework.

Quickly, I thought of something to cover up my lie. "Yeah, I needed to use a computer, but they're all being used right now. I was just going to wait for a bit until one opened up."

"Oh, okay. Well I can wait with you then," Luke smiled, putting his hand over mine.

"That's silly, you don't have to wait here with me and waste your lunch hour," I said, moving my hand away from his.

Luke looked at me for a moment, then began to get up from his seat. I sighed in relief as he started to walk away. Just when I thought I was home free, Luke turned around the corner of the table and took a seat next to me.

"Is everything okay?" he asked, clearly worried.

"Yes, everything's fine," I said, not making eye contact.

"Are you sure? You can tell me," Luke said softly.

"I'm sure," I said, making eye contact, trying to convince him.

"Okay then," Luke said, grabbing my hand and giving it a gentle squeeze. "If you ever need to talk, I'm here." He leaned in and kissed my cheek.

"Thanks," I smiled weakly.

Luke just sat and stared at me for a while. I couldn't stand this. I cared so much about Luke and I wanted to tell him everything. I couldn't tell him though; it was killing me inside. I knew that look on his face; he was worried. He was in pain. He didn't know whether to persist or leave it be.

"Looks like a computer is free now," I said, changing the topic and getting up from the table.

"Yeah," Luke sighed, getting up from his seat.

"I really need to get this English essay written."

"I guess I should let you get to that then. I won't distract you anymore." Just like that, Luke was gone again.

As soon as he disappeared into the hallway, I pulled out my phone and texted Carsynn.

To Carsynn:
From Julie:
Do you want to skip the last half of the day and just hang out?

I hit send and I received a reply almost instantly. I told her I'd meet her out by my truck. I got up from the computer and headed out to my truck.

"What's up?" Carsynn asked when I got to my vehicle.

"Well, I think that I'd rather spend time with you than be in class," I laughed, hopping in.

"I completely agree," Carsynn smiled, climbing into the passenger seat.

"So where do you want to go?" I asked.

"Hmm, mini-golf?" Carsynn asked, crossing her fingers.

I couldn't help but laugh. Starting the ignition, we headed towards the mall. "Yes, we can go mini-golfing."

"Yes!" Carsynn cheered, punching the air with her fist.

Carsynn turned on the radio and immediately began to belt out the lyrics to the song.

We both sang together at the top of our lungs. By the time the song was over, we were gasping for air.

"Man, I miss these moments," Carsynn sighed, turning down the volume.

"Yeah," I laughed, "me too."

"Hey, can I ask you something?" I asked, pulling into the mall parking lot.

"Absolutely, what's up?" Carsynn asked.

"What do you think of Luke?"

"He's a great guy. I can tell that he really cares about you," Carsynn smiled.

"I care a lot about him too, it's just, I don't know what to do," I sighed, parking the truck.

"About what? What you two have is wonderful. Why mess with it?"

I hesitated before continuing, "I don't think it's fair to him to be dating me."

"Why not?" Carsynn asked, shocked.

"I can't be honest with him," I sighed.

"Julie, c'mon. You're making this harder than it needs to be," Carsynn started. "We can help you get out of this situation, you've just got to let us."

"It's not that eas-" Just then, I saw my father walk across the parking lot into the mall. "Shit, we've got to get out of here."

"Why? What's wrong?" Carsynn asked, looking around.

"My dad, he's here. He just walked into the mall." I started up my truck again and got out of there as quick as possible. "Let's just go back to my house."

"Okay, we'll watch a movie or something," Carsynn sighed, putting her seatbelt back on.

"Sorry Carsynn. We can still going golfing another day," I smiled.

"You can count on it," Carsynn laughed. "I love mini-golf."

"Yeah," I agreed. "I know you do." I pulled into my driveway and parked the truck. We sat there for a couple of seconds before making any movement.

"I think I'm going to break it off with Luke," I blurted out, opening the truck door.

"Julie, you know that's not a smart decision to make," Carsynn said, pulling me back into the truck. "He makes you so happy."

I turned to face her, "it's the only way to keep him safe. My father is constantly threatening me to keep my mouth shut. Every time I get close to anyone, he reminds me of the consequences. If my dad knows I'm not hanging out with Luke anymore, he won't be suspicious." We hopped out of the truck and headed downstairs to my room.

"I still don't think it's a good idea."

"Let's just change the topic for now?" I asked, slipping into more comfortable clothes.

"Yeah sure, what movie do you want to watch?" Carsynn asked, moving over to the DVD rack.

"Hmmm, pick something funny," I suggested, looking over the DVD's as well.

"No way! You have Step Brothers?" Carsynn screamed, reaching for the DVD.

"Yes, yes I do," I laughed, sitting down on the couch.

"We are watching this, no arguments," Carsynn said, popping the disc into the DVD player. "Are you hungry?"

"Help yourself," I laughed, "I'm not too hungry."

"Well, I will do just that," Carsynn ran up the stairs. "Don't start without me!"

"Don't worry, I won't." I sighed and pulled out my phone. There was one message from Luke.

To Julie:
From Luke:
Where are you??

I quickly sent a message back.

To Luke:
From Julie:
Carsynn and I decided to hang out for the rest of the afternoon

To Julie:
From Luke:
Miss you :(

I didn't even bother replying to the last message. I didn't even know what to say to him anymore. I realized that I was hurting him by practically ignoring him, but he would be hurt more if he found out I was being abused at home by my own father. I was doing the right thing. At least I hoped I was doing the right thing. It had to be the right thing.

Watching Step Brother's helped me get my mind off of things. I couldn't stop laughing. It was honestly, the funniest movie I had seen in a long time. Carsynn and I decided to watch movies for the rest of the day. About half way through Finding Nemo, I drifted off to sleep.

"Why didn't you tell me?"
I looked up to find Luke standing over top of me. "I couldn't Luke, you have to understand. He would kill me."
"I can't let him keep hurting you," he said, moving towards the doorway.

"Luke, wait! He'll kill you too," I sobbed, reaching for his arm, trying to stop him.

"No. Julie, I love you. And I can't stand by while you get hurt all the time." He left my room and headed upstairs where my father was doing paperwork. Screaming and yelling erupted from the floor above. I tried to get up and help Luke, to try and save him. But my body wouldn't let me. It was like my body was shutting down. Nothing was working except my tear ducts. All I could do was cry, and hope that Luke would be okay. I heard a gun shot and then the sound of a body crashing against the floor.

The next thing I knew, I was standing beside a hole in the ground. I peered into the hole and saw a wooden coffin; I was at someone's funeral. I looked around, trying to find Luke. I didn't see his face anywhere. Instead, I spotted my father, glaring at me. Luke had died; he was trying to save me. This was all my fault.

"Julie, get up," Carsynn said, shaking me awake.

"Huh?" Sitting up, I realized I had been crying.

"Are you okay?" Carsynn had a worried look on her face.

"I'll be fine," I sighed, wiping the tears from my face.

"You keep saying that, but I don't think you are," Carsynn said desperately. "You need help. Honestly, you can't solve this on your own. I know you don't want me to help, but I'm going to, whether you like it or not."

"What? No. Please Carsynn, just let it be. You'll just make it worse," I begged. "They're just nightmares."

"He fractured your shoulder Jules," Carsynn exclaimed

"It'll be healed in two weeks, just leave it be," I snapped as I got up and went to my room. I immediately felt terrible for the way I was treating Carsynn. All she wanted to do was help. "I'm sorry," I sighed from the doorway. "I'm just a little crabby."

"It's fine Julie, I shouldn't be poking into your business," Carsynn said, pulling me in for a hug, "but I want you to know that I'll be here when you're ready to get out of here."

"Thanks," I smiled, shocked at Carsynn's sudden change in attitude. "I'm kind of tired, I think I'm going to hit the hay. Goodnight."

"Night Julie," Carsynn smiled.

The next couple of days went by very quickly; it was already Friday. Carsynn would be leaving tomorrow morning. I had done my best to put my problems to the side and enjoy the time I had left with Carsynn. We went mini-golfing after school one day and we went out for dinner afterwards. We also went shopping at the mall and bought a couple of cute outfits.

"I'm going to miss you," Carsynn said as she sat down on my bed.

"I'll miss you too," I smiled.

"I just wish I could stay here longer," Carsynn said, a tear rolling down her cheek.

"Hey, it'll be okay," I said, reaching in for a hug. "We'll still write each other and call each other."

"I know," she sniffled. "I'm just worried about you."

"Don't be," I sighed, "I've handled this sort of stuff since my mom died. I can handle it for a couple more years until I turn eighteen."

"You shouldn't have to though."

"It's okay, just don't worry about it."

"Whatever you do, don't break up with Luke, okay?" Carsynn said.

"Why?" I asked, changing into my pajamas.

"He makes you happy," Carsynn said, "I can tell he does. I know you think it's not fair to him, but it's not fair to you either. Why get rid of something that makes you happy? Especially considering the situation you're in."

"I'll think about it," I replied, curling up into bed. "We should probably go to bed, you've got to get up early tomorrow."

"You can say that again," Carsynn moaned. "It should be illegal to get up before the sun shines."

"I'll miss this," I laughed. "Goodnight Carsynn."

"Night Jules."

"Do you have everything?" I asked, grabbing my truck keys off of the counter.

"I think so," Carsynn sighed, taking one last look around. "If I forgot anything, you can Fed Ex it to me."

"Yeah, sure thing," I laughed. "C'mon, you're going to be late for your flight." We headed out the door and were on our way to the airport by five.

"If you ever need to talk, call me," Carsynn said, getting out of the truck.

"I know, I know," I laughed, "you're here for me."

"I am!" Carsynn said. "Remember what we talked about last night."

"Don't worry," I sighed. "I'll be fine."

"Okay," Carsynn said, grabbing her suitcase. We headed towards customs where Carsynn and I would say our final goodbye.

"Give me a hug," Carsynn pouted, opening her arms. I reached out to Carsynn with my one good arm and gave her a hug.

"Call me when you get home," I said, a tear rolling down my cheek.

"Of course," Carsynn smiled, glancing down at her watch. "I better go."

"Probably a good idea," I laughed. "Bye Carsynn, I'll miss you." We gave each other one last hug before Carsynn walked towards Customs.

"I'll miss you too."

I stood there until Carsynn was on the other side. When she was through Customs, we waved goodbye to each other for the last time. After that, she was gone.

The ride home was very quiet; a familiar feeling. It was a feeling I had not felt for a while. Oddly enough, it was comforting. Ever since I moved to Philadelphia, I hardly had any alone time.

I couldn't help but think about what Carsynn had said. I was making things harder than they needed to be. Sure I could tell everyone about my secret, but then everything would change. Everyone would look at me differently. My dad would obviously go on a rampage. I would probably end up moving again before he got into any serious trouble. My life would become a living hell once again.

On the other hand, I could just keep my secret to myself. I could keep dating Luke, not telling him my secret. Usually, I didn't have any trouble lying about my injuries, but with Luke it was different. It was hard to lie to him. I always felt guilty afterwards. I could break things off with Luke, and I wouldn't have to lie to him. He would be able to move on and I wouldn't have to hurt him. Sure, it would kill me to let him go, but I needed to do the right thing.

So those were my choices. Tell everyone my secret with a small chance that I would get out of this situation. Or I could just keep my mouth shut and break up with Luke. It was pretty obvious what I needed to do. I just had to figure out how to do it.

CHAPTER 11

It's been two weeks since Carsynn left. I've gotten rid of the sling; all evidence of my shady secret has disappeared once again. The only thing left is a bit of soreness. I was sitting in the living room when there was a knock on the door.

"Jules?" I heard a familiar voice say.

"I'm in the living room," I sighed. This was it.

Luke walked around the corner and sat down on the couch next to me. "Is everything okay?"

"Yes," I replied, turning towards Luke.

"What is it then?" Luke asked, grabbing my hand.

"I need to talk to you," I sighed, taking a deep breath. "I uh-"

"Are you breaking up with me?" Luke asked, suddenly letting go of my hand.

"No," I sighed, "definitely not."

'Then why have you been avoiding me?"

"That's what I'm trying to tell you," I said, looking down.

"Sorry," Luke apologized, grabbing my hand yet again.

"This isn't easy to say," I started. "There's some-" I stopped mid-sentence when I heard someone walk through the front door.

"Julie," my father called out.

"Dad, hey," I said, getting up from the couch. "I thought you were gone for the weekend."

"I wasn't feeling good, so I came early. Is there a problem with that?"

"No, none whatsoever." I sat down on a stool by the counter.

"Ah, hello Luke," my father smiled as Luke walked in behind me. "I didn't realize you were here."

"Hey Mr. Baxton. How's it going?" Luke smiled, taking a seat beside me.

"Feeling a bit under the weather," he shrugged. "I'm going to take a nap."

"Hope you feel better," I said. With a shrug and a grunt, he headed up the stairs to his room.

"So what was it you were going to tell me?" Luke asked, turning to me.

"Nevermind," I sighed, "it wasn't that important."

"Well obviously it was," he insisted, "you called me all the way over here."

"Yeah, I know. Now just isn't the best time anymore."

"Let's get out of here then," Luke smiled.

I nodded in agreement and we headed out the door hand in hand.

"So what was it you wanted to say?"

"Okay," I sighed, "I'm just going to come out and say it." We reached the park and sat down at one of the benches.

I took a deep breath, unsure of what was going to happen after this. "You remember those injuries I had?"

"Well yeah," Luke said, "what about them?"

"They weren't exactly . . . accidents."

"What do you mean?" Luke asked, worry spreading across his face.

"Ever since I was eleven," I said, a tear rolling down my cheek, "my father has . . ." I couldn't bring myself to say the words. Now that I was about to tell the truth, I couldn't help but feel embarrassed. I didn't even have to say anything else. Luke pulled me into a hug and just held me. He didn't say a word as I sat there in his arms and cried. The weight that had been on my shoulders since I was just a little girl had finally been lifted.

It was at that moment that I knew everything would be alright. I just had this gut feeling. "I'm a mess," I sighed, wiping away the last tear.

"You don't deserve this Jules," Luke sighed. "I'm not going to stand by and watch it happen."

"You have to," I sighed, sitting up again.

"Why? He's hurting you! You can't expect me to ju-"

"Please?" I asked. "I only told you because you deserve to know. I can't bare lying to you all the time." Luke had an expression on his face that told me he was going to put up a fight. "Just leave it, otherwise he'll hurt you too."

"I'm willing to pay that price," Luke said, getting up.

"Where are you going?" I asked.

"I'm sorry Jules, but I just can't let this happen." Luke grabbed my hand as he started walking away.

I pulled my hand away and stood my ground. "Luke," I pleaded. "If you confront him, you'll ruin everything." The tears began to stream down my face again.

"Jules," he sighed. "Please let me help you."

"You're only going to hurt yourself," I sobbed. "We can't win. Just leave it."

"C'mon," Luke sighed, "I'll take you home." He walked back towards me and put an arm around my shoulder. "I won't say anything."

I put my arm around his waist and we walked back to my house in silence.

"I'll always be here for you," Luke smiled as we reached the door.

"I know." I kissed Luke on the cheek and went inside, "Thanks." Luke nodded as I closed the door behind me.

"What was that all about?" I jumped at the sound of my father's voice.

"Nothing," I said quickly, making my way towards the stairs. "I thought you were going to bed?"

He ignored my question. "Why were you crying then?"

"I uh-"

"You told him, didn't you?" he said, cutting me off.

"Told him what?" I asked, trying to look innocent.

He moved towards me and yelled, "you know exactly what I'm talking about!"

I couldn't help but shrink and look towards the floor. "N-no I didn't."

"Liar!" he shouted. "You're going to pay for this!"

I braced myself for what was to come and shut my eyes tight. Instead of feeling the usual pain, I heard a big thud and opened my eyes in time to see Luke knock my father to the ground. I stood there in disbelief.

"I won't let you hurt her anymore!" Luke yelled at my father. "I heard everything you said to Julie, and I have it all on tape." He held up his phone and hit the play button.

"You're going to pay for this!" Luke stopped the recording and took a step towards the door.

"You're not going to get away with this," he said, looking down at my father who was still on the floor. "C'mon Jules, let's go." He turned towards me and reached out his hand towards me.

Before I could say anything, my father was off the floor and running towards Luke. I tried to warn him, but it was too late. All I could do was scream Luke's name.

He turned around just as my father's fist connected with his jaw. The force was so great, Luke was knocked down to the ground. My father continued to beat on Luke, kicking him repeatedly in the side; his stomach contracting with each blow.

"Dad," I pleaded. "Stop it!"

"This is your fault!" my father yelled, kicking Luke one last time. "Pack your bags. We're moving again."

My instincts took over and I moved towards Luke instead; he was barely moving at this point. "Luke?" I whispered, trying to get a response.

"I said pack your bags," my father yelled.

"I have to make sure he's okay," I whispered, leaning over Luke.

"Leave him! "My father ripped me away from Luke's still body. "Hand over your phone. I don't want you blabbering your mouth to anyone else.

"He needs an ambulance!" I cried, taking my phone out of my pocket.

He took the phone out of my hand and pushed me towards the staircase. "Pack light."

I took one last look at Luke before I ran down the stairs to my room. I rushed into my closet. My duffel bag was already packed; it was always there for emergencies like this. I grabbed the duffel bag and tip toed up the stairs. I looked around to find my father already gone. I rushed over to

Luke, knelt down beside him, and whispered, "I'm going for help. Please, stay strong. I love you."

I got up off the floor and headed towards the front door. I took one last look at Luke before turning the doorknob.

"Where do you think you're going?" my father asked, spotting me from the top of the stairs. Just my luck.

"I thought you were outside," I lied, opening the door wider.

"Well you were mistaken," he spat. "Close the door."

I took another glance towards Luke; he was so helpless. I wanted to run and get help for him. I looked back towards my father who was now at the bottom of the stairs. I hesitated at the doorway.

"If you want Luke to stay alive, I'd suggest you close the door now."

There was no way out of this. I couldn't run anymore, even if I wanted to. My father was too close and there was no doubt that he would catch me if I tried. I closed the door slowly and set my bag on the floor.

"Good choice," he smirked, grabbing his bag off the floor. He walked towards me and picked my bag off the floor. "Let's go."

"What about Luke?" I asked, looking at his now unconscious body.

"Don't worry about him," he laughed. "Someone will find him."

"We can't leave him like this!" I exclaimed, walking towards Luke.

"Quit your complaining!" he yelled, grabbing my arm and pulling me back. "We'll call someone when we get out of here!"

A tear fell as my father dragged me out of the house, slamming the door behind us. The sun had set and it was almost pitch black outside. "Where are we going?" I sobbed, getting in his truck.

"Chicago." My father started up the engine and we drove. We had been driving for half an hour when he handed me his cellphone. "You can call someone now."

I called the only number I knew could help. I stated the address to the 911 operator, "and send an ambulance, quick." I hung up the phone and handed it back to my father. "You're not going to get away with this."

"Watch me," he laughed, merging onto the I-76, heading west.

I tried to catch some sleep but I couldn't clear my mind. This was all my fault. I never should've listened to Carsynn. The reason I had kept all of this a secret for so long was to avoid this exact situation. Luke was hurt, and it was because of me. To top it off, I would never know if he was okay.

We didn't make any stops on our way to our new life. It was roughly a thirteen hour trip.

"We're going to have to start all over because of you," my father said, glaring in my direction.

"This isn't my fault," I spat. "You're the one that's hurting me."

"And you're the one that couldn't keep her little mouth shut." We pulled up to a car rental shop. "Your new name is Paige Lawrence and I'm Daniel Lawrence. Your mom ran off to Hawaii with a man when you were four. We just moved here from New York."

"Is that everything?" I asked, looking out the window.

"You know, you're lucky I planned for this."

"Whatever," I sighed, "can we get this over with?"

"Gladly."

I spent the next couple weeks getting settled into my new life. Of course, I couldn't walk around looking like Julie Baxton. My father insisted on a new look for me. I booked an appointment with the local salon for a haircut and a dye. My father also insisted that I go tanning at least twice a week to darken my skin tone. After everything was finished, I was no longer a blonde, but a brunette. My long hair had been chopped off and replaced with a bob. When I looked in the mirror, it wasn't my reflection I saw, but a complete stranger's. The old Julie Baxton was gone.

"Julie, listen to me when I'm talking to you," my father spoke up. I sat up quickly and looked in his direction.

"Now that I have you're attention," he sighed. "You're going to be home schooled from now on. Clearly, I can't trust you to stay quiet anymore."

"What? Please no," I pleaded, "I'll stay quiet. I promise!"

"You're going to be home schooled, end of discussion," he said, taking a seat at the kitchen table.

I couldn't believe this was happening. Not only was I going to be home schooled, but now I had no escape from my father. I was stuck in this house all day. On the bright side, I wouldn't have to deal with being the new kid once again.

"And seeing as you don't need your facebook anymore, I deleted it for you," my father smiled, taking a sip of his coffee.

"Why am I not surprised?" I sighed, heading to my new room. "This isn't going to work. My friends are going to come looking for me."

"But they won't be able to find you," my father laughed. "Don't even think of trying to contact them either. Otherwise we'll just have to do this all over again."

"I hate you."

*   *   *

It's been two months since we left Philadelphia. I've left my house a total of three times; once for the mail, once for groceries, and another to pick up a book from the library. My father doesn't allow me to leave the house unless it's absolutely necessary. He runs most of the errands nowadays. I don't know how much longer I can bare this. My life is equivalent to hell.

"Paige!"

"What?" I asked, realizing he was talking to me. My new name hadn't sunk in quite yet.

"Have you finished reading that book for English yet?"

"Yeah," I replied. "The book report is done too."

"Good," he said, walking into the kitchen. "You can bring it back to the library, but be back in half an hour."

"Okay," I said grabbing my bag and running out of the door. I loved moments like this; times where I could enjoy the fresh air. The library was only ten minutes away, I didn't know why he gave me half an hour, but I was not about to complain.

I got to the library, dropped my book in the return box and headed back out to the fresh air. I checked my watch; twenty minutes to spare. I definitely didn't plan on going home early. I decided to stop by a little coffee shop on my way back. I stepped inside the door, heading straight for the counter.

"Hi," the girl behind the counter smiled. "What can I get for you today?"

"A small coffee please."

"One small coffee coming right up," she said. "That'll be $1.45"

I reached into my bag and grabbed my wallet. Crap, I didn't have any change. "Is it okay if I use debit?" I sighed, taking out my debit card.

"Well sure," she smiled.

I paid for my coffee and headed back home. I made sure to drink my coffee before walking through the front door.

"Paige, there's someone here to see you," my father called out as I shut the front door. "We're in the living room."

I racked my brain to think of anyone who might visit me; nothing. I hadn't talked to any of my old friends since I'd left Philadelphia. No one knew where I was.

"Hi Paige," the stranger said as I walked into the living room. It was a man who was about thirty years old; he was wearing a grey suit.

"Hi?" I said, confused.

"This is Mr. Martin," my father smiled. "He'll be your new teacher."

"Huh?" I asked, still confused.

"I've been offered a job. Therefore, I won't have the time to teach you anymore. I've hired Mr. Martin to take my place."

"Okay," I said slowly. "It's nice to meet you." Mr. Martin got up off the couch and stretched his hand out towards me. I grabbed it and shook it weakly.

"You as well," he smiled, handing me a piece of paper from his briefcase. "This is an outline of your new schedule."

"Great," I sighed, looking at the sheet.

"I'll be here every weekday starting tomorrow. Lessons will run from ten o'clock until three o'clock. You'll get a half an hour lunch break. I also expect you to have all your homework done on time."

Well this guy seemed like an easy going fellow. Just when I thought life couldn't get any worse.

"Don't worry, my daughter is a very hardworking kid," my father said, putting an arm around my shoulder. "She'll get her work handed in on time, won't you Paige?"

"Yeah," I smiled. "Absolutely."

"I'll see you tomorrow then," Mr. Martin smiled, heading towards the front door.

"Goodbye," my father waved. "Thank you."

"Anytime. Goodbye now." The front door shut and Mr. Martin was gone.

"Try and keep your mouth shut this time," my father said, dropping his arm from around my shoulder.

"Whatever," I sighed, heading towards my room.

"Don't walk away from me," my father shouted, grabbing my arm and pulling me back.

"Ouch! What?" I yelled, "what else could you possibly say?"

"I'm warning you Julie." My father threw me towards the ground.

"I got that the first time," I snapped. "God, I really hate you."

"Don't worry," he laughed. "The feeling is mutual."

"Go to hell," I said, getting up from the ground. I went to my room and fell onto my bed. It was already six o'clock; dinner time. I couldn't bring myself to even think about food right now.

I missed Luke; I missed him a lot. I missed hanging out with Mark, Ella, and Carsynn. I missed my old life. I wished there was some way I could get in touch with everyone and let them know I was okay. Of course, there was no chance of that. Nowadays, internet access didn't even exist for me. All I could do was hope that Luke was okay and that one day someone would find me.

In the morning I would have to deal with Mr. Martin. God only knew what he had in store for me. I guess the up side to having Mr. Martin as a teacher was that I wouldn't have to deal with my father on a daily basis. That was one positive thing in my life. I fell asleep that night feeling sorry for myself.

"Mr. Baxton! Open the door!"

I rolled over in my bed and looked at the alarm clock. It was seven in the morning. "My god," I sighed, getting out of bed.

I plodded down the hall to the front door. I was about to turn the door handle when my dad whispered from the kitchen. "Don't open the door!"

"Why?" I said aloud.

"Keep your voice down," he whispered, motioning for me to join him in the kitchen.

"Mr. Baxton! This is the police! Open the door!"

"The police?' I exclaimed, joining my father. "What's going on?"

"I could ask you the same question, you little brat." He opened a drawer and pulled out a gun. He pulled me into a headlock and pointed the gun at my head. Then I realized why they were here. The officer had said 'Mr. Baxton' instead of 'Mr. Lawrence'. Somehow they had found us; we had left a trail.

"Dad," I pleaded. "I swear, I didn't tell anyone anything."

"Obviously you did," he spat. "Now you're going to pay for it."

Just then, the front door was knocked down and five police officers rushed in.

They didn't even have to search the house; we were found immediately.

"Sir, put the gun down," one of the officers said.

"Dad, please," I cried. "You don't have to do this."

"Shut up!" he screamed, tightening his grip.

"Mr. Baxton. There's no way out of this," the officer said. "Just let your daughter go and no one will get hurt."

"Where does that leave me?" my father exclaimed, "I'll go to jail for who knows how long. I won't let that happen."

"Mr. Baxton, you can't win in this situation. Either you go to jail and pay for your time," he said, pausing. "Or you can kill your daughter and get twenty-five years to life. It's your choice."

"This is what we're going to do," my father said. "You're going to put your guns down and you're going to let Julie and I leave through the back door."

"Sir, the house is surrounded. It doesn't matter which door you leave through, you will be caught."

"No, I won't. You're going to tell your team to back down. Now." My father tightened his grip even more; it was getting harder to breathe.

The officer hesitated before putting down his gun, causing the rest of the team to lower their weapons as well. "There," the officer sighed. "But we aren't going to back down until your daughter is out of harms way. Give us your daughter and you can get away."

"No, that's not how this works!" My father yelled, "Julie comes with me!"

Suddenly, the sound of a gun shot pierced my ears. I slipped out of my fathers grasp and fell to the ground. I felt a weight land on top of as soon as I hit the floor.

The officers rushed towards the chaos and I found myself being dragged out from underneath my father. "Are you hurt?" I heard one of them say. I didn't have an answer for him.

Everything was happening so fast; nothing was clear. My eyesight blurred as I was rushed out of the house and into the daylight. I could make out a crowd of people surrounding my house. There were red and blue lights flashing. Someone called out my name, "Julie!" Before I could recognize the voice, the daylight started to fade and I plunged into darkness.

CHAPTER 12

This isn't your fault. This isn't your fault. This isn't your fault. The words kept replaying over and over. There was nothing else; just those four words. This isn't your fault. Then I heard it; a faint whisper. Someone was calling my name. Julie, Julie, Julie. It kept getting louder and louder.

"Is she going to be okay?"

"She'll be fine. She's just in shock."

Were they talking about me? What had happened?

I opened my eyes just a crack to find myself in the back of an ambulance.

"Julie," I heard a familiar voice sigh in relief. I knew that voice; it was the voice I had been longing to hear for so long.

"Luke?" I opened my eyes wider to find him sitting at my side. I couldn't help it; I reached up and wrapped my arms around his neck. "Oh Luke," I sighed. "I'm so glad you're alive!"

"Jules," Luke smiled, "of course I'm alive."

"I'm so sorry," I cried. "I didn't mean for any of this to happen."

"I know, I know," Luke sighed. "It's not your fault."

"Yes it is. If I would've kept my mouth shut, none of thi-"

"Jules, it's okay," Luke comforted. "It's all over."

"What happened to my dad?" I asked, suddenly remembering what had happened back at the house.

"Well," Luke started. He went in to detail about what had exactly happened and why I got out of there alive.

An officer had snuck in through the back door and crept up behind my father and I. When my father's anger started to escalate, the officer had no choice but to eliminate any chance of me getting harmed. The officer shot my father in the shoulder, allowing me to get away safely.

"Is my dad okay?'" I asked, looking at the paramedic.

"Your father was taken to the hospital. The doctors will patch him up and he'll be just fine," the paramedic stated.

"So what happens now?" I asked, "where does he go after that?"

"Your father will be brought to jail where he'll await his trial."

I couldn't help but sigh in relief; it really was all over. I turned to Luke to get some more questions answered. "How did you guys find us anyways?"

"You used your debit card," Luke laughed. "Your debit card was the one thing your father forgot about."

"What?" I asked, completely confused.

"When you use your debit card, the police can find out exactly where and when it was used." Luke grabbed my hand and squeezed it.

"I bought a coffee yesterday," I said. "My dad usually gives me money, but I wasn't supposed to be buying anything."

"Well, it's a good thing you were craving a coffee," Luke laughed.

"No kidding," I sighed.

After all this time, the weight I had been carrying for so long was finally gone. I didn't have to worry about my father anymore. I couldn't help but feel exhausted.

"You should try and get some sleep," the paramedic smiled. "You've been through a lot."

I didn't have to be told twice; I drifted to sleep as soon as my head hit the pillow.

The next time I woke up, I was laying down in a hospital bed; Luke was at my side, holding my hand.

"How was your sleep?" Luke asked, noticing I was awake.

"Peaceful," I smiled.

"The doctor said you were free to go whenever you woke up," Luke said, kissing me on the forehead.

"Where do I go?" I asked, realizing that I no longer had a home to go to. "Where am I going to live?"

"Don't worry," Luke said, rubbing my hand. "We'll figure something out."

I spotted my clothes on a chair beside my bed and got changed. These hospital gowns were drafty; too cold for my liking.

"Thank you," I said to Luke as I walked out of the room. "I owe you."

"Nah," Luke laughed. "It was the least I could do."

I linked my fingers with Luke's and we walked down the halls towards the exit together.

"Julie!" I heard an angry voice call out. I turned around to find my father in cuffs, walking towards me with two officers. "You'll pay for this!"

"C'mon," Luke said, rushing me outside. "You'll never have to see him again." I took one last glance at the man yelling at me before I walked out the front doors.

*   *   *

We landed at the Philadelphia International Airport around two o'clock in the afternoon.

"Home, sweet home," I said, walking out of building and into the sunlight. I spotted Luke's mom and waved at her; it was good to see familiar faces. Luke grabbed my bags and put them in the trunk as I hopped into the vehicle.

"How are you dear?" Luke's mom asked, starting up the ignition.

"Never better," I smiled.

The ride home was very quiet and peaceful. It gave me time to reflect on everything that had happened over the past three months.

I had spilled my secret, Luke almost got killed, and I moved away to Chicago. My old identity was erased and I became Paige Lawrence. I was under house arrest for two months until I was finally saved by my debit card. My father was going to jail and I could finally live my life without being shadowed by constant fear. Things were finally looking up.

"We're here," Luke smiled, interrupting my thoughts.

I looked out the window as we pulled into Luke's driveway. Mrs. Hecks parked the car and I got out of the vehicle, stretching my legs.

"C'mon," Mrs. Hecks smiled. "Let's go inside."

Mrs. Hecks and Luke grabbed my bags, motioning me to go on inside. "We'll follow you in," Luke smiled.

I walked up the front sidewalk and pushed the door open. I reached for the light switch and flicked them on.

"Welcome home!" Mark, Jake, and Ella screamed. Luke and Mrs. Hecks came up behind me and repeated the phrase. "Welcome home."

I stood there in disbelief as they all ran towards me and gave me a group hug.

"I missed you guys," I sighed, choking on my words. A single tear fell down my cheek. This time, a tear of happiness.

"Wait a minute," Jake said, holding his hands up.

"Luke," Mark started, "I think you brought the wrong girl home."

"Yeah man," Jake laughed, pointing at me. "This isn't our Jules. Our Jules had blonde hair."

"Oh shush, you two," I laughed, wiping away the tear.

"Some things never change," Ella laughed, pushing through the boys and giving me a big hug. "I'm glad you're back home."

I smiled, returning the hug, "me too."

"Hi Julie!" Heather piped up, running into the room. "I am so glad you are back! We have all been so worried and Luke can't stop talking about you an-"

"Okay kids, give her some space," Mrs. Hecks interrupted. "The poor girl is probably exhausted."

"You're right," I laughed weakly. "I should probably catch up on some much needed sleep."

"You can sleep in the guest room for now," Luke smiled, picking up my bags.

"It's nice to see you too," I smiled at Heather as I followed Luke down the hall.

"This is it," Luke smiled, putting my suitcase in the far corner. I rushed over to Luke and wrapped my arms around his body. I never wanted to let go of him again. We embraced each other for what seemed like an eternity. This is when the real tears began to fall.

"I never want to lose you again," I sniffled.

"Don't worry," Luke said, taking a step back and holding my head in his hands. "I will never let anyone hurt you again."

"You almost died," I whimpered. "My father almost killed you."

"But he didn't," Luke smiled.

"But he alm-"

Luke leaned in and silenced me with kiss. He broke away and smiled, "I love you."

"I love you too," I smiled, putting my father to the back of my mind.

"You should get some rest," Luke said, giving me one last kiss.

We broke apart and I sat down on the bed. "Good idea."

"One last thing," Luke said, stopping in the doorway. "Carsynn's going to call you tomorrow morning. She knows you're safe but she has been so worried about you."

"I wouldn't doubt it," I yawned. "She's probably going insane."

"Sweet dreams," Luke smiled, shutting off the light and closing the door.

For the first time in a long time, I had no trouble falling asleep. I felt at home and nothing could bring my mood down. Everyone was safe and sound. My father was behind bars and I was back in Philadelphia with my friends and my amazing boyfriend. Of course, I never imagined my life to end up like this. I figured that my father would always be around, ready to strike without warning. Now I knew that wasn't the case anymore. The rough times had finally ended. As soon as my head hit the pillow, I was out like the light.

CPSIA information can be obtained at www.ICGtesting.com
Printed in the USA
LVOW060117040512

280259LV00001B/1/P